Fritz and the Blink

An Overture to Life

By

John R. Cohagen

PublishAmerica
Baltimore

© 2005 by John R. Cohagen.
All rights reserved. No part of this book may be reproduced, stored in a retrieval system or transmitted in any form or by any means without the prior written permission of the publishers, except by a reviewer who may quote brief passages in a review to be printed in a newspaper, magazine or journal.

First printing

ISBN: 1-4137-5275-6
PUBLISHED BY PUBLISHAMERICA, LLLP
www.publishamerica.com
Baltimore

Printed in the United States of America

— About the Author —

John Rogers Cohagen was born in 1948 in the small rural East Texas town of Overton. His dad was a postman and his mother was a high school English, speech and drama teacher. He loved acting from his first role in Billy Goats Gruff in Kindergarten. He continued acting through junior high school, high school, and college and later in the Henderson Civic Theater.

Life for John was always interesting, though not always pleasant. Married and divorced before he was out of college for a full year, he later married again and this year celebrates thirty-one years of happiness.

He taught high school biology and science for 5 years in Caldwell, Texas, before going back to college for a master's in Building Construction Management from Texas A&M University. He worked commercial construction and residential remodeling for about 6 years before becoming a computer bookkeeping manager for a sign company. Four years later he started his own sign company in his old home town. The company went bankrupt after 10 years when John Quixote fought the windmills of local politics.

Following a short stint as a city councilman and a few months of unemployment, John once again went into construction as a superintendent. The company kept him out of town for 365 of the 390 days he worked for them, so he left the job, preferring to starve than being away from his family. He worked as a field superintendent for three more years with another company. After being laid off due to a construction lull, he took the time to write this book. He then worked again in construction as a field engineer, and he has no regrets for his choices

John has a loving and understanding wife, Sharon, three children, John Jr., Joshua, and Jennifer, and one grandchild, Holden Michael. He feels that all the problems he may have had in his life were worth it when he sees the children he has raised and knows that they will always be together, for all were raised to love the Lord. John never had any ambition to be rich and has to this point in his life succeeded in that regard; but like George Bailey in *It's A Wonderful Life,* he is the "richest man in town" when he has his family around him.

— Dedication —

The knowledge that this book would be written has been with me for many years. Why I waited so long is a mystery. I often used the excuse that I had to wait for my parents to pass on because some of the things I wanted to include in this book were embarrassing to me in my child-parent relationship. Looking back, I know now that my parents already knew almost all of the stories I am going to tell and they treasured each of them as much as I do. After all, in a town as small as Overton, Texas, there are no secrets to be kept.

They possessed several special qualities that made it possible for my brother and me to explore all the offerings of life: love, patience, understanding and trust. They raised Jim and me to be very independent, curious, and self-confident but respectful of our elders, the law, and other people's property and to treasure our heritage as freedom-loving Americans. They gave us ample opportunity to make our own mistakes, but saw to it that we learned from them. If it were not for their particular type of parenting, this story would never have been possible. It is to the memory of those two wonderful people, Lillian and Arnold Cohagen that I dedicate this book.

Mom and Dad with Fritz and the Blink.

— Table of Contents —

Introduction — 11
Prologue — 14
Chapter 1 Our Family Heritage — 19
Chapter 2 The Times and The Town — 24
Chapter 3 Times Before John — 32
Chapter 4 The "Blinky" Experience — 37
Chapter 5 Our Early Years — 42
Chapter 6 Getting a Bang Out of Life — 58
Chapter 7 Special Events — 71
Chapter 8 The High School Years — 80
Chapter 9 Testing the Limits — 102
Chapter 10 The Things That Made Us Laugh — 114
Chapter 11 Pranks and Practical Jokes — 124
Chapter 12 Sleds, Skis and Scooters — 139
Chapter 13 Jim's College Years — 148
Chapter 14 A Tribute to Friends — 156
Chapter 15 Don't You Laugh
            When the Hearse Goes By — 162
Chapter 16 The Other Side of the Story — 169
Chapter 17 It Takes an Attitude, Not a Village — 177
Epilogue — 185

— Introduction —

I count myself fortunate for the experiences I had growing up in a small East Texas community where life was slow and the people were kind. Here in the middle of the "Bible Belt" I learned many valuable lessons about life, love and family. Everyone in town was your neighbor and it seemed that everyone knew you by name. It was a far cry from the hustle and bustle of the big city and yet, though rural, was not like life on the farm.

The times had a lot to do with this; it was the early fifties and World War II was still strongly embedded in the minds and hearts of those who had lived through that tragic and difficult time and the Great Depression that preceded it. Many of our citizens had been "over there" and carried the scars, both mental and physical, of the struggles they had been through. There were also many fresh graves in our local cemetery of those who had given the ultimate sacrifice for their country so that we could enjoy the freedoms which we still claim as Americans.

The Fourth of July was celebrated with picnics in the park and fireworks. Thanksgiving was truly a time to remember and give thanks for the blessings we had received. Christmas, of course, was the highlight of the year with parades, food and, naturally, fireworks.

The Cohagen family had been in the area since 1900 and four generations are now buried in the Overton Cemetery. My paternal grandmother's family, the Arnolds, had been in this immediate area since 1854 and descendants of that family were scattered all over the area.

JOHN R. COHAGEN

The city of Overton was on the edge of the East Texas Oil Field when it was discovered in the early 1930s. It grew into a boom town during the Great Depression sheltering those who lived here, and moved here, from the really "hard times" that the rest of the country was suffering through. However, being on the edge of the field, the oil played out rather rapidly. The population soon moved northward toward the center of the field, leaving Overton behind. By the time I came along in 1948, Overton had been reduced once again to a small town of about two thousand and has remained about that same size to this day. Empty buildings remain as reminders of the numerous businesses that once flourished there.

As a child, I remember there were five automobile dealerships; today there are none. We had three movie houses; today there are none. There were three pharmacies filling prescriptions for four doctors; now only one of each remains. The hospital where I was born was closed in the sixties and after going through many varied ownerships is now the capital building for the Republic of Texas, a group that believes that Texas should not be a part of the United States, but rather a separate country (so they won't have to pay income taxes). I have always wondered if the room where I was born is now the office of the President of the Republic of Texas, but I have never bothered to find out.

However, in spite of the changes, Overton remains my home today, and I live in the house where I grew up. I left for about twenty years and lived in central Texas where I attended Texas A&M University, taught school, and worked at various jobs in the field of construction. Returning home was not easy, for while many of the same buildings and people remained, the influx of new blood had given the city a completely different flavor. Many of the businesses I had grown up around were no longer in existence, many new faces filled the streets, and most of the friends I had grown up with had moved on to bigger and better things.

Yet I still live in the memories of the city I knew in my childhood. It was a wonderful place; filled with friendly neighbors, many kinfolks and an atmosphere most conducive to raising children. I brought my young family back here to raise them as I had been raised, but I learned all too quickly that you can never really go home.

That is another story entirely, so I must now re-focus on the one I have to tell. The story of growing up with my brother, Jim Cohagen, in the small rural community that in my memory was perfection, at a time when my life was filled with love and excitement and where opportunities abounded for youngsters who were willing to explore the limits of living. To do this, I would like to take a little time to introduce you to my family, our little town, and the times that made my memories so dear to me. I hope you can reminisce a little with me (if you are of that age) or learn a little from me (if you are too young to remember the '50s) about the way life was when I was a child.

— Prologue —

As I have grown older, the years of my youth have become more precious to me, and the memories of those wonderful years have become the "good old days" to which we all long to return. I find myself at that point in my life where places ache that didn't before, stairs are steeper, loads are heavier, and running is only a mental exercise. The memories of my youth, however, are vivid and sweet; though I sometimes have a problem remembering what happened yesterday. I am the last survivor of the family that nurtured me. I am no longer the baby of my family, but now the patriarch of my family; the father of a new generation, and the grandfather of yet another. I only hope that I will be as good in that role as the grandfathers of my past generations were for me.

The story you are about to read I lived with my blind brother, Jimmy. Wonderful parents, grandparents and kin surrounded us. Jimmy was an incredible older brother who overshadowed my youth. He left in his wake a life of accomplishments so outstanding that I often felt I was being compared to him and always losing. Strangely, at the time, I didn't mind all that much because I also believed that my big brother was one of the most awesome individuals I had ever known and was proud to be a part of his truly unique life. Looking back, I feel that because of the kind of brother I was, I helped him become what he most wanted to be, independent.

This book attempts to relate the experiences Jim and I shared growing up in a world that always looks better when looked back upon. Some of the things we did were truly stupid; others were pure genius. Some of the things would probably land us in jail if they were done today. None of our antics, however, were founded on malicious intent, just the spontaneous products of two uninhibited youths with extremely active imaginations and the opportunities afforded by the times, the small town and the understanding family in which we lived.

Parts of this book contain information from Jim's autobiography, written in high school as a senior English term project. I was aware of the project when he wrote it, but since I grew up with him and thought I knew it all, I never read it. Now some forty years later, after both of my parents and my brother have passed on, I discovered his work stored in an old chest in which my mother kept her most personal memories. His paper was entitled, "An Overture to Life." As I read it for the first time, I discovered there were aspects of my brother's life that had never been shared with me including a good rendition of life in the family before I was born. It helped to fill in gaps of my memories and complete the story I wanted to tell. I have used a few quotes and many paraphrases from his book that give insight to who he was and how he viewed himself and the world around him. As he stated on the title page to his life story, "Any similarity between persons described in this book and persons living or dead is purely intentional."

The introduction of his project concluded: "It is hoped that this book will be enjoyable as well as interesting. If this is so, then it has accomplished the purpose for which it was written." My purpose reflects that sentiment. I do not pretend to be a great author, only a person who enjoys writing and taking the opportunity to share what I consider to be a unique childhood in the hopes that you, the reader, will enjoy that experience.

I don't know exactly when I became aware that I even had an older brother. By the time I was two and a half years old, Jim had already started attending the School for the Blind in Austin. For all practical purposes, I was an "only child" for nine months out of the year. Mom had started teaching when I was only six months old and I was left in the hands of our colored housekeeper / baby sitter for most of the day while Mom and Dad worked to earn the money needed to keep the family going. Our housekeeper had a son who was four and a half months older than I was, and we spent much of our early years growing up together. So much so, that I thought of him as my brother. I certainly had more contact with him than I had with my real brother.

I don't even know when I became aware that Jim was different than other kids. It was never really an issue. Jim was blind; some people are. To me, he was just my brother and playmate when we were together and nothing was ever thought of his blindness. He didn't make it an issue, and I accepted it as normal.

Jim would come home from school for the summer, Thanksgiving and Christmas. I know that we spent as much time as possible together during those times and I learned to read by spelling out the comics in the newspaper and comic books and having the words pronounced by Jim. We would giggle and laugh together, reading books, telling jokes, singing funny songs. We loved to laugh and talk and sing. This often continued well into the late hours in our shared bed until being threatened within and inch of our lives by our parents who were trying to sleep in the next room.

In the summers we were a real family. Mom was not teaching, Jim was at home and Dad was the only one who had to work. As a substitute mail clerk, he worked very early or very late and was at home with us a lot during the day. We had a very close-knit family structure and often went to our grandparents' farm where there were many things for kids to do. Our grandfather, Papaw, was a retired mail carrier. He had carried the mail in a horse and buggy for many years, but now he was a gentleman farmer. He and his wife, Mamaw, lived in her father's house after he died and received a fair income from oil royalties from her father's estate. They were both Godly people and from them we gained a real understanding of love—love of God and love for each other.

The farm abounded in aromas. The smell of horse manure, dried corn in the corn crib, and the musty smell of stacked hay were always present. The old house itself had a smell all its own, partly musty, partly the smell of the vegetables that were stored under the floor on drying racks. Potatoes, onions, corn and other vegetables were readily available under the house. The freshly cut grass and the newly plowed ground added the finishing touch to the symphony of smells we enjoyed there. We could ride the sled behind Papaw's mule, Old Ella, or we could run freely in the fields and woods around the house. This was a child's paradise where the imagination was the only limiting factor to the amount of fun a kid could have.

This was, of course, East Texas and in the summer, shoes and shirts were optional for kids and rarely worn. The soles of our feet, toughened by the gravel driveways and black-oil streets, soon became so calloused that the sticker burrs would not penetrate them except in the tender arch or between the toes. Suntans were achieved within the first week of summer and remained as evidence of the summer fun well into October.

But the greatest part of summer in our family was the annual family vacation. Dad had traveled during the time he was in the Army Air Corps in World War II and loved everywhere he went. He had old Army buddies all over the United States, and he kept in contact with many of them by mail and telephone for many years. To be able to see them and also to help his family enjoy life, he had set a goal to take the family to all forty eight of the contiguous states. By the time I was twelve ears old, he had achieved that goal for the family.

Every summer was different. Dad would map out a route to take in as many previously unvisited states as possible within the two-week vacation time allowed. We would stuff the family into the car along with everything we could carry: tents, food, cold drinks, cameras, clothes, swimsuits and all the necessary items to enjoy the sights we were going to enjoy. We had an old stainless steel Dr. Pepper® soda fountain dispenser box that served as our ice chest. In that we carried sandwich meat and all the condiments. Often Dad would build a platform covering the tunnel in the floorboard of the back seat to make it a flat place where we could sleep.

Being from a very small town, we were easily impressed by the size of the world that was outside our little East Texas universe, but at the same time, being among the few in our town who had ventured so far and wide and experienced the whole United States, we were not easily impressed with the things that happened at home. Partly because of this experience, Jim and I were challenged to create more excitement in our otherwise quiet little burg.

This book tries to recount the special relationship Jim and I shared, not only as brothers, but as friends. We were two brothers with ample opportunities to use our creativity, our curiosity, and our mischievous natures to their full extent. We were also bound by our total disregard for conformity, choosing our own way of expressing ourselves, often disregarding logic and good sense. For children of our time, we lived on the edge of the envelope. We were free, we were independent, and we were invincible.

All in all, the time I shared growing up with Jim was the most memorable part of my life. I hope that the time you share with us as you read our story will be memorable, too. I also hope that reading a book about a young blind boy's struggle to be accepted as normal in a seeing world will provide inspiration to other people who are facing hard times or handicaps in their lives. For those readers who have a normal life, I hope it provides you with the opportunity to look inside yourself and question your perception of those who are struggling with their difficulties. Jim often expressed his belief that the hardest thing about making new friends was their hesitance to accept him as normal and getting comfortable being around him. The incorrect perception of and reaction to his blindness were often stumbling stones for those who met him for the first time.

Most of all, I hope that you will enjoy reliving with Jim and me the joys of our youths in a simpler time and the struggle to discover who we really were and what we might become.

I intentionally included very few pictures in this book. The mental pictures you conjure up will be better than all the photographs I could provide. So sit back, relax and make yourself comfortable as the orchestra of your imagination tunes up for *An Overture to Life*.

— Chapter 1 —
Our Family Heritage

Our family was neither rich nor poor; comfortable would best describe our position in life. Mom and Dad both worked to provide that comfort. At one time, for a few months, Dad held down four different part-time jobs simultaneously to make ends meet. He was a substitute mail sorter at the post office, an insurance salesman, operated a miniature golf course, and was a photographer. Mom was a school teacher, high school English, speech and drama. Mom was the budgeter and bookkeeper and could account for every penny we spent and saved. Having been raised during the Great Depression, money had a special meaning to both of my parents. They knew the value of money, though they had no plans of taking any of it with them when they died. They believed that money was worthless unless it was spent to improve and enjoy life or unless it was being saved for emergencies or used to help others. They always had money for their tithe at church, for their favorite charities, and donated regularly to our local black church.

Mom's side of the family could be traced back indirectly to President James Buchanan, though her personal claim to fame was that Jack Wrather, multimillionaire producer of the *Lassie*, *Lone Ranger*, and *Sergeant Preston of the Yukon* TV series, was her second cousin. Recently, I began to study my genealogy and discovered that her maternal grandmother's family led to a treasure trove of kinfolks that she never knew about including Kings of Ireland, Scotland, France and England. Some lines are traceable to William the Conqueror, Charlemagne and three Revolutionary War soldiers.

Her maiden name was Rogers and while we would like to claim we were related to Will Rogers, such was not the case, though her father could twirl a rope better than Will himself. She was born in Rogers, Arkansas, and we kidded her unmercifully about being a hillbilly, though she was quite refined and well educated. She moved to Overton, Texas, with her family during the depression because the East Texas oil boom offered jobs and opportunities for her father to support his family.

Dad, on the other hand, was born, raised, lived and died in Overton. Except for a few years during World War II, he never lived anywhere else. His mother's family, the Arnold family, had lived in this area since the early 1850s. Roots could be traced back to Henderson County, Tennessee, where his great-great-grandmother was born in 1776 as well as two generations farther back to Virginia, the Revolution and England. The first Arnold in America fought at the Battle of Yorktown, saw the surrender of Cornwallis, and the birth of our nation. Having ancestors directly traceable to colonial times before the birth of this nation, I proudly call myself a *Native American*. The Arnold family can also be traced back indirectly to Benedict Arnold and, on another branch, indirectly to Francis Scott Key, who wrote "The Star Spangled Banner."

His dad's paternal family only dated back to 1858 when his grandfather was born in Jefferson City, Missouri. At age twelve his grandfather, John Marion Cohagen, ran away from home and came to Arkansas, then Louisiana and later to Corsicana, Texas. He finally arrived in East Texas around 1900, and lived in Overton until he died in 1935. Very little is known about his grandfather, as he would never talk about his life before coming here or the reason he left Jefferson City and his parents. It was rumored in the family that he rode with Quantrill's Raiders after the Civil War and later with the James-Younger gang. There is even one family story that claims that Frank James came to Overton and stayed at his home. None of these rumors have ever been confirmed

Among other things, John Marion was a farmer and merchant in Texas during the early 1900s. He had lived in Corsicana, Texas, moved to Roan, to Old London, to New Salem, later to Seven Pines, and Price. He finally moved back to Old London, Texas. Each time he had the same bad luck. Someone would discover oil on his land and the drilling and crude oil would destroy his farmland. He would sell out and move to a new location. Oil was basically worthless in those days, only a few cents a barrel, so he never kept any of the mineral rights to the land he sold. If he had, I would never have had to work a day in my life.

Dad's maternal grandfather had better luck. When he left home, he moved to New London, then known as Norfolk, where he had a general store and farm. When oil was discovered there, he sold off all but eighty-five acres of his four hundred and fifty-acre farm but he kept one-eighth royalty rights on all minerals. He was able to enjoy the rest of his life in comfort and public service. Oil wells in that area still bear the name of J. H. Arnold and still produce income for some of his heirs.

Some of the land he sold off in New London bordered the site of the New London School that exploded on March 18, 1937, killing some two hundred and ninety-eight students and faculty. My wife's father lost a brother and had a sister injured in the explosion. It was believed the explosion was caused by a natural gas leak in the basement that was ignited by a spark from a light switch. It prompted the addition of an artificial odor to natural gas, which naturally has no odor of its own, so that leaks could be readily detected in the future.

J. H. Arnold's daughter, Ethel, married my grandfather, Ed Cohagen, or Papaw as we called him, and they moved in with J. H. Arnold after his wife died because he was in poor health and needed someone to care for him until his death. They lived on the farm until Ethel had a stroke and was paralyzed. Much of our growing up was done on that farm, as it offered wide-open spaces and a myriad of opportunities to explore the natural world. Papaw had a mule named old Ella that my brother Jim and I rode behind in a sled designed for gathering corn from the fields.

Mamaw and Papaw were two saintly people. No one who ever knew them could recall a time when they raised their voices at each other in anger. Papaw always had a song or a poem to share, and Mamaw cooked the best chicken and dumplings in the world.

My mother, Lillian Rogers Cohagen, "Lil" to her friends, Mrs. Co to her students (including her own two children when we were at school), taught English, speech and drama at our high school for thirty-one years. She had lived in Overton since 1932 and everyone knew her. Anything my brother and I did, she would hear about from friends or students, but nothing we could do would surprise her.

Mom was only five feet two inches tall, but in the eyes of her students, she was seven feet tall. She was a stern but fair disciplinarian who bragged that she never spanked a single student in the thirty-one years she taught. She did have one weapon at her disposal that could cower the largest of men: the respect her students and friends had for her; respect that she earned by respecting others. She could give a look that would melt the soul. Just knowing that look meant disapproval was enough to rein in the most obnoxious behavior.

At home, Mom, not Mrs. Co, was a different person all together. She was sweet, kind, understanding, and loving; but she was still a strict disciplinarian who could not boast that she did not spank her own children when they needed it. She was not stingy, much the opposite, but she was extremely frugal with our funds spent on necessities to ensure that ample funds were available for our pleasures.

Dad was much different. He was jolly, outgoing, humorous, and the most unselfish person I have never known. He loved to spend his money on his wife and kids. He always had a joke or humorous story to tell and never met a person he didn't like or wouldn't talk to. Humor was his forte, compassion was his soul and his family was his life.

Dad had an aura of calm about him at all times. He faced every aspect of his life with the same tranquil demeanor. Be it joy or tragedy, celebration or strife, good times or bad, Dad always had the same calm, patient and loving manner. I believe he knew his Maker better than most and knew very surely that everything was under God's control, so he didn't have to waste his time worrying about it.

One of our parents without the other would have only been ordinary people, but the combination of both of their personalities created the greatest home any child could ever hope to be born into. All the guidelines for growing up were there: strength, discipline, compassion, humor, and trust. Most of all there was love and the dedication to each other that gave our family the strength to face all of our troubles together and the faith to know that all would be well with the help of God.

I included this background of our family to help you understand the heritage of the two youngsters with whom you are about to make acquaintance in this book. It is important to understand that we were from a very close family, steeped in humor, with pride in who we were and love for each other and the Almighty God who many times blessed us and protected us, often from our own foolishness more than outside forces.

— Chapter 2 —
The Times and the Town

Life for a youngster in rural East Texas in the 1950s was very different from what it is now. World War II was over and soldiers were returning home to re-establish their lives. New homes were popping up like mushrooms after a spring rain, new families were being created, and the "baby boom" generation was being born.

After the war, Mom and Dad moved back to Overton and with the help of their parents, they built a small five-room home, which soon had to be added on to as I prepared to make my appearance in this world. It would continue to grow to meet our family needs for years to come. Now it has nineteen rooms on five levels under thirty-five hundred square feet of roof. What once was a huge yard for kids to play in has now become quite small as the house has taken up more and more of the surface area. I have no real problem with that because it is much easier to mow and take care of a smaller yard as I am growing older.

My Haunted House

Each of the rooms has its own deeply implanted history that haunts my memory from time to time. All of the rooms have been remodeled now. Most of them have been remodeled by me. The process of remodeling involved stripping away layers of previous work, revealing reminders of times past and creating pictures in my mind of how it was back then. One bathroom, added in the first remodel that took place just before I was born, had four layers of wallpaper and one layer of paneling. Stripping the layers away in succession, I could remember each motif, the way the bathroom looked when that particular layer had been there and the way I viewed them and life at those different times. It was fun to reminisce about how I viewed the world differently when the walls were covered with pink flamingoes and green marsh grass on a black background. Life was beautiful then, but that bathroom was *U G L Y*!

I Have to Reminisce

That was in the early fifties when cold drinks were only a nickel and candy bars were a nickel, too. Twenty-five cents would treat a kid under twelve to the movies with enough left over for a coke and a bag of popcorn. You could buy a little box of Spanish peanuts for a nickel and every once in a while, you would find a nickel, a dime or even a quarter inside. The family could go to the Jersey Queen, the local hamburger joint, and get five hamburgers for a dollar delivered to your car by a friendly carhop. Gasoline was nineteen cents a gallon and as our tank was being filled, the attendant would check the tires, oil, and radiator, as well as wash our windshield, all the while smiling.

Life was much slower paced and much less complex. We had four doctors in our small town and an office visit was only three dollars. If you were really sick, they would make house calls with their little black bags. The "pet" frogs that Dr. "Heigh" kept in his office always fascinated me. How was I supposed to know they were used for pregnancy tests? In fact, the word pregnant was never used in polite conversation or around children. A pregnant woman was "with child," "in a family way," or "going to have a baby," but she was never *pregnant*.

Our telephone number had only four digits to remember – 6-9-7-1. You placed long distance phone calls by calling an operator, a live human operator, who would connect your call for you. To call Mamaw in the next town, you only had to dial "9" and her four numbers. We had to go to the post office to get your mail from our post office box in the lobby, ours was Box 237, or if you lived outside the city you could have it delivered to you on rural route. Home delivery didn't come about until the mid '60s. Post cards were two cents and a stamp for a letter cost three.

We slept with our windows open at night with an attic fan pulling fresh night air across our beds. We didn't worry about whether we had locked the doors or not; people trusted their neighbors and respected their property and privacy. We were lulled to sleep by the sound of "old squeaky," an old oil well about five blocks from the house, as it droned out an eerie song of squeaks and clanks as it pumped oil from the ground. If it ever stopped pumping during the night, the roar of the silence would startle us from our peaceful slumber.

The sounds of trains switching cars on the sidetrack downtown stirred our imaginations and we would speculate on the origin of the freight cars and where they might be bound. We enjoyed watching the old steam engines when they would stop in town to take on water from the watering tower near the tracks. By the late fifties, the arrival of the diesel locomotive spelled the demise of the watering tower. Our mail to and from out of town traveled on a train known as "the Eagle" as it sped through our town every night at nine o'clock. The Eagle never stopped in Overton except for the one time when someone put a dummy on the tracks and the engineer thought he had run over a real person. I was sometimes allowed to accompany an old gentleman named Mr. Leonard as he would take the outgoing mail packed in heavy canvas bags with large brass locks to a special rack by the side of the tracks. The sack was hung on the arm of the rack prior to the arrival of the train. There it would be snagged by a big iron hook on the protruding from the side of the mail car and thrown violently into the open door on the side of the speeding train. Another big canvas sack that contained the incoming mail for our post office would be thrown like a bag of garbage from another door of the mail car to the side of the tracks where it would roll and tumble to a stop in the tall grass. Mr. Leonard would retrieve the sack and take it to the post office.

FRITZ AND THE BLINK: AN OVERTURE TO LIFE

You could set your clock by the arrival of the Eagle, and there were usually people sitting by the tracks every night to watch it speed by, watching the busts of passengers framed by the aluminum windows in the lighted cars like a mobile art gallery. One of our many local characters would sit by the tracks every night, waiting for the Eagle to bring his wife back home. It mattered little to him that she had died many years before.

Small circuses, gypsies in wagons and even medicine shows would sporadically come to town for our entertainment. We had three movie theaters, remnants of the boom days when Overton was a thriving town on the very edge of the East Texas oilfield in the thirties. The main part of the oil field was actually north of town around Kilgore, which had oil derricks all over the downtown area. At one time, there were twenty-eight oil wells, complete with derricks, on one city block. That block was to become known as the "World's Richest Acre." As the limits of the oil field moved that direction, the population that had moved into Overton so rapidly began to trickle out to follow the work.

How We Have Changed

In those days, pot was something you boiled vegetables in, Coke was a soft drink in a 6 1/2-oz green glass bottle with a penny deposit, income tax was a whopping four percent, and sales taxes didn't exist.

The mushroom-shaped cloud that had ended World War II had created a bonanza for filmmakers. The idea of mutants created by nuclear radiation filled the screens with oversized creatures of every shape and description. There were bees the size of horses, ants that were eight feet long, huge spiders, flies, crabs, grasshoppers, praying mantises, and the one that gave me the willies, stinging scorpions as tall as a house. UFO reports and science fiction movies kept us all looking to the skies and wondering if life really existed "out there." To this day I love to watch *The Day the Earth Stood Still*.

Radio was still very popular. We listened to *Edgar Bergen and Charlie McCarthy*, *The Green Hornet*, *Jack Benny*, *Amos and Andy* and *Gun Smoke*. Television was just making its appearance, and it wasn't until around 1958 that we got our first set. Early televisions had round screens and the view was usually as much static and interference as picture, but it caught on fast.

An elderly couple that lived next door had the first "color" TV I ever saw. Actually it was a black and white set with a piece of thin, transparent and tinted plastic that was stuck onto the screen; a blue tinted strip at the top to simulate sky and a green tinted strip at the bottom to color the grass, and there was a flesh colored strip in the middle where people's faces should be. It was kind of neat when you were watching an outdoor scene, but it gave Howdy Doody and Buffalo Bob a truly strange complexion. It made me think that all television houses had blue ceilings, green carpet and yellow walls.

Antennas sprung up on the roof of almost every home. Sunday nights were special with *I've Got a Secret*, *The Ed Sullivan Show* and the *Wonderful World of Disney*. I would rush home after school to see the *Mickey Mouse Club* and like every kid of my time, I fell in love with Annette Funicello.

The advertising of the time was often more entertaining than the programs; my favorites being the old Jax beer commercials with the talking cartoon dog. "Dizzy" Dean gave the All-American game of baseball a new language of its own with his drawl and mutilation of the English language, and Russ Davis from ringside in the Amphitheater in Chicago, with his gift of gab, made us believe that professional wrestling was truly REAL.

There were fewer people in the world back then and we had much more free open space to explore. Life was fun, simple and as exciting as your imagination could make it. Sex was not mentioned around children, violence was news not entertainment, cowboys got shot but never bled and alternate lifestyles were not acceptable alternatives. The news actually reported what had happened without telling you what you were supposed to think about it.

People were friendlier, the pace of living was slower and God was in our lives and schools on a daily basis. Patriotism was taught in schools where God was welcome. Our founding fathers were still considered to be heroes who founded this nation under God, and in 1954 our Pledge of Allegiance was changed to reflect that view. Joe McCarthy was seeing communists behind every tree, and the government was not so intrusive in our daily lives.

It was a great time to be growing up, especially in a small rural town, far away from the problems of big city life. The developing drug culture was limited mainly to the pot-smoking beatniks in New York and Los Angeles.

A Trip to the Barber Shop

You could get a haircut back then for a quarter. And the barbershop was the center of all local gossip. My great uncle Eaph (rhymes with leaf), who had been the town marshal during the rough and rowdy days of the oil boom, was the first barber I ever knew. Every other Saturday, Jim and I would be taken to his shop, placed unceremoniously on a padded board that straddled the arms of the barber chair and *subjected* to a haircut. The favorite haircut for kids was the "burr," which was to peel all the hair on the head down to one-quarter inch or shorter. From the phonograph in the corner came the words and music of a big favorite of that time: "Put another nickel in, in the nickelodeon, all I ever want to hear is music, music, music."

There was no wiggling allowed in the barber chair and head position was not optional. Uncle Eaph had very large hands, best described as ham hocks, and he was less than gentle in turning your head to the position *he* wanted it to be in. I was told that as marshal, he slapped an uncooperative lawbreaker unconscious with a single swipe of his huge, open hand. Judging by the immense size of his hands, I believed it. His shelves were lined with bottles of hair tonic in an endless variety of colors, smells and shapes. A good dowsing of Three Roses hair tonic would immediately bring any unruly hair under his control.

Men could get a good shine on their shoes while waiting for their turn in the barber's chair. A black man named Toby had his bench in the shop with a chair mounted on a high wooden box with iron foot rests where his work was done. There were drawers underneath the rests with all his waxes and rags. I used to love to sit and watch Toby shine shoes; it was a source of fascination. Toby would sing as he worked, cleaning off the shoes, applying the wax. Then he would use a long, folded rag to bring the waxed leather to a deep shine, snapping and popping the rag in time with his song. A shoeshine by Toby was not just a shine; it was a performance.

Some Things Have Changed for the Better

One of my uncles had a Texaco® station right in the middle of town. Back then, service stations had three restrooms: MEN, WOMEN, and COLORED. That was always confusing to me. I was taught there were only two sexes. White folks sat on the ground floor of the theater and black folks were obliged to sit in the balcony that was accessible by a separate entrance. Swimming pools, though public facilities, were white only, and the few cafes that would serve both black and white had separate non-connected dining rooms with separate entrances. Even the doctor's office had separate waiting rooms. All of this was very confusing to me, having been raised with a black maid and friend. We continued to play together for many years on the weekends, at his house, at mine and at my grandfather's farm after the segregated schools of the time separated us during the week. I was in second grade before I learned that there was an "r" in "Califonia." This would all change in the next ten years or so, and one day I hope to write a book about those times and the changes as they viewed through the eyes of this child growing up, but that is another story and hopefully another book.

In a small town, everyone knows you, they know your parents and your family, and they care. If you got out of line, they didn't call the police; they called your dad and he made you wish they had called the police.

This was the atmosphere in which my brother and I were raised, in a family that knew the meaning of love, discipline and responsibility to God and country. I firmly believe that all of these factors were necessary to allow the events that shaped our lives to occur.

— Chapter 3 —
Before I Arrived

World War II was winding down. Dad was stationed at Majors Field in Greenville, Texas. Dad was a Corporal in the Army Air Corps, serving as a photographer and cartographer. March 21, 1945, brought spring to Texas, and on the same date, a stork flew over Majors Field and delivered an eight pound, four ounce bouncing baby boy, James Arnold Cohagen, Jr.

Three months later, Dad was discharged from the service and the family moved to Kilgore, Texas, where they opened a photography studio. Times were tough after the war and for a short time Mom and Dad lived with Dad's parents, until they, with the help of both of their parents, were able to build a small, five-room house in Overton, which would quickly and forevermore become a home.

Some time before Jim was one year old my parents began to notice that he did not respond to light as he should. One day, while talking to Jim in his crib, Mom noticed a gray spot behind the pupil of his eye. After several visits to the local doctors, they advised them that he should go to Dallas to be checked by specialists. Here the family would receive the news that Jim had tumors forming in both eyes. The disorder was known as retinal blastoma, a genetic cancer that had spontaneously developed while Jim was still in the womb. The prognosis was that with immediate radiation treatments Jim would probably lose only his sight, even though the survival rate for that disorder at the time was very low.

Radiation treatments were begun immediately. Twice a week, the family had to make a trip to the hospital in Dallas, some 100 miles away. They were very difficult for Jim, because he had to be held perfectly still for several minutes while the radiation was focused on his eyes from the side. They were even more difficult for Mom who had to hold her frightened and struggling infant while the treatments were being given.

The treatments were quite serious, time consuming, and ultimately failed to save Jim's sight. On Monday, March 23, 1946, just two days after his first birthday, Jim had his left eye removed. After that, the family continued to drive to Dallas every other day for continuing treatments to save the right eye. This also failed to be successful, and at the age of 20 months, Jim had his right eye removed.

As a result of the radiation treatments, Jim bore serious radiation burn scars on the sides of both eye sockets. In one respect the treatments had been a success, for Jim was the first person to have this form of cancer to live past the age of twelve. In fact, he never had any recurrence of that cancer the for rest of his life.

Though Jim admitted that he had no actual memory of the treatments, he once became very frightened when he was young when he heard a sound that reminded him of the high-pitched noise that the x-ray machines had made.

You Cannot Lose What You Never Had

Some would consider the loss of vision by a child to be a tragedy, but Jim recalled in his book, *"Actually, to use the word loss, when speaking of what little vision I had is to overstate the facts considerably. At best, my vision was poor, and it had been necessary to learn to get along without it long before the operations."* His lifestyle was not seriously cramped by the loss, and Jim continued to develop pretty much the same as he had before the operations. He admitted that he really didn't have any idea that he was any different from anyone else and did pretty much what other kids his age were doing. Since the house was so small, Jim had little trouble finding his way around and soon was running around the house like any other toddler, getting into everything and bumping into very little.

Jim's First Best Friend

The family acquired a long, brown Dachshund, which was named Snuffy. I think this was after Snuffy Smith in the comic pages, because that was one of my dad's favorite strips. At any rate, Snuffy became Jim's best friend, and they were almost inseparable. For Jim, Snuffy was playmate, doll and surrogate brother.

Celebrate Birthdays All Year Long

Jim never let his lost sight interfere with his life. For him it was just the way God intended for him to be, and he accepted that without question. He grew into a typical two-year old, very social and very out-going. He loved birthday parties, his own and any other he could be invited to. He recalled, *"Of course, my own were my favorites, but since they came only once a year, I had to rely on other people's to fill-in in the meantime."* He especially enjoyed eating birthday cake and opening presents, even if they happened to belong to someone else.

Very early in life, as soon as he learned to talk, Jim admitted that he developed foot in mouth disease. As with most kids, tact is an unknown concept, and they often repeat what their parents say at a time that it was not intended to be said. Jim's first vocal blunder was memorable and was retold for years throughout the family.

Near our house lived a kindly widow who had chosen selling Avon® products as her profession. She was a bit of a nuisance as she peddled her wares, coming to visit at inopportune times and often overstaying her welcome in order to make a sale. She also would babysit for our parents and was very close to the family. However, on one occasion, Dad and Mom were discussing her in front of Jim, and Dad made the comment that sometimes she was a bit of a pest.

Not long after that, the lady came by the house to sell some Avon. Jim took that opportunity to share his recent discovery. "Are you really what my daddy says you are?"

"Why, I don't know, honey. What does your Daddy say I am?" she asked.

Before Mom could gag him, Jim announced, "Well, he says you are a pest."

Mom could not prevent the slip. About the best she could do was to send Jim out of the room and try to make the best of the situation. I don't know how much make-up she bought that day.

The Duo is Complete

On February 27, 1948, I joined the family. Jim always claimed I had been mixed up from the first day I was born. In the first place, Mom and Dad couldn't figure out what to name me. Mom loved alliteration and wanted to call me Corky Cohagen, a name that I still remember Jim calling me on occasions when he wanted to make me mad. I was lucky to be a boy, because I could have been Candy Kane Cohagen. Dad thought John was a good name, named for my mother's father, John Ophus Rogers. The battle raged for a while, but John Rogers finally won out. However, as parents have a way of doing, the name they give is not the name they use. John became Johnny. The battle raged for years to come, John or Johnny. I detested the name Johnny, preferring to be called John, because it sounded more mature and was, after all, my true name. Fifty-five years later, there are still those who grew up with me who call me Johnny. Now it is proudly accepted, because it immediately identifies friends of my youth.

Six month later my grandmother Rogers, Mom's mom, died. I never remembered her, but Jim often told me that she was very kind and, as far as he could remember, very cheerful. He also claimed that she was the best pie maker in these parts.

With my impending arrival, the little, five-room house began to be a little small, so during the fall of 1947, the job of adding onto the house began. To a two-year-old like Jim, this certainly seemed to be an enormous task. There were huge piles of wood, huge tools, and men doing large amounts of noisy work. With all this huge stuff around, it is lucky that no one got hurt. About the most serious accident to come of the building was when Jim fell through the floor.

The carpenters who were building a new bathroom had cut a hole in the floor where the shower was to eventually be installed. Not knowing this, Jim decided to go inspect the job after the carpenters were through for the day. He searched all through the room and was just about to leave when it happened. Plop, he fell through the hole and onto the soft, sandy ground below. He found himself hopelessly stranded in a hole he couldn't get out of. He had to call for help, which didn't arrive soon enough for him. He wasn't hurt, but by the time he got out of that hole, he was pretty upset about the slow response time that his mother had exhibited in his time of crisis.

I Will Not Be a Fake

Sometime during Jim's early life, Dad acquired a pair of glass eyes for Jim. They were gray-blue, like Jim's eyes had been, and very natural looking. I can remember several occasions when Dad tried to insert them, but Jim fought them and Dad was never successful in getting them in place. I don't know if they were that uncomfortable or whether Jim was just being stubborn, but after only a few attempts, they were put in a drawer and never mentioned again. I truly suspect that Jim simply did not want to have them, as they were not what he really wanted was. They certainly wouldn't give him sight, and they wouldn't fool anyone into thinking he could see. Jim had no problem with the fact he could not see, and if it bothered someone else, that was not his problem.

— Chapter 4 —
The "Blinky" Experience

The loss of his eyes and one grandmother and the addition of his little brother and his favorite friend, Snuffy, had made life for Jim quite interesting. However, Mom and Dad recognized that Jim would soon have special needs in the area of his education and that there was nowhere in the immediate area where Jim's needs could be met. They had heard about the Texas School for the Blind in Austin, and it seemed to be the best idea. They had considered sending Jim to public kindergarten, but for some reason never did. In retrospect, Jim wrote, "That might not have been such a bad idea; because it seems to me that I was a much better mixer at that age than I am now." We will never know how that decision might have affected his early development, but Jim never really gave the choice much thought.

When Jim was five, Mom and Dad took a trip to Austin to check on the State School for the Blind. Evidently they liked what they found out, for they returned home full of optimism, which they shared with Jim. Consistent with his adventurous nature, he took to the idea immediately, thinking, I'm sure, that it would just be another great adventure for him.

In September of 1951, Dad and his father took Jim to Austin to enroll him in the School for the Blind. The experience was one that Jim would never forget.

Texas State School for the Blind

I was only two when Jim began attending Texas State School for the Blind, so by the time I was able to walk and talk, I no longer had a full-time brother and for nine months out of each year. I was, for all practical purposes, an only child.

This was Jim's first time to be away from the family for any extended length of time. He recalled that the first couple of days he was too busy making new friends and exploring the new environment to be homesick, but on the third day, he and many of the new students cried to go home but couldn't. He was stuck at "the Blinky," on his own for the duration.

The school was affectionately known to the students as "The Blinky." There Jim would learn all the things a blind person needed to know to become a fully functional *blind* person. Jim had a problem with that, because he never thought of himself as blind, only that he could not see, and he detested the connotation of the word blind as it represented a limiting factor for life. He never wanted to be a functional *blind* person; just a functional person. To Jim a totally blind person was a "Blink," not to be confused with the "Bats" who resided in the Texas State Mental Health Hospital, "The Bat Hatchery," just across the street. The use of the term Blink now would, of course, be considered politically correct and insensitive, but this was the '50s and politically correct phrases like "visually challenged" had not been coined yet; though I am quite sure Jim would have had a ball with that euphemism as well. After all, his vision wasn't challenged, it was non-existent, and no amount of sugar coating would change that fact. If he could accept that, why couldn't the "normal" people?

For the next eight years, Jim attended the Texas State School for the Blind, learning to read and write Braille, studying the usual elementary and junior high school subjects, learning social skills, and preparing for life. He also learned to play piano, guitar, violin, and to wrestle.

Elementary School

Early classes included modeling clay, bead stringing, weaving and other things that were done with the hands to keep their young minds occupied. The children had books and stories read to them to develop their language skills. The following year he was taught to read and write Braille. Learning to read a bunch of dots with my fingers would seem an impossible task, but Jim always said it was no harder than it was for me to learn to read. First you are taught to recognize the alphabet, then to recognize and spell words, then to put the words together into phrases and finally sentences. This is the same way any sighted child learns to read only it is done with the tips of the fingers instead of with the eyes.

For the first three years, the students were housed in cottages with children their own age and pretty well isolated from the older students. A cottage might contain as many as twenty-eight students living in rooms with up to eight kids. In the cottage the students formed gangs or "camps," as they were called. Within the camps there were leaders and followers, and between the camps, there was rivalry and fighting. Camps were not promoted, but they were tolerated because they taught team spirit and cooperation. Jim told me many stories about fights between rival camps in those early years.

One of my favorite stories relates how his camp decided to take control of a situation that was affecting their play area. Jim told it like this:

"*Although there was usually some feuding, fighting and fussing going on between the camps, there was at least one common enemy, an obese cook who worked in the cottage kitchen. We got particularly upset with her when she parked her car in what we called the summerhouse. This was nothing more than a super-sandbox, which must have measured about ten feet long and eight feet wide, covered with a wooden roof, about six feet high. At any rate, we considered this summerhouse strictly off limits for obese cooks, and it sure got our dander up when she insisted on parking there. It didn't take long for our contriving, young minds to come up with a great strategic move. It would be best, we decided, to dig holes in the sand just behind her back wheels and, in spite of the chance of getting caught, we got right to work. The results of our labor were amazing. The cook had a lot of trouble getting her car out of the summer house, and after a few more treatments, she was completely cured of parking her car in there."*

I include that quote from Jim's autobiography to illustrate a certain trait of his personality, which I feel was very important in the development of his future self. We would call him a control freak today, but he was only considered stubborn at the time. He had, however, developed the desire to control his own environment and future. It would be this desire that would govern many of his decisions as he grew toward manhood.

After the third grade, the students were housed in dorms with age ranges of three years. In that way the students got to learn from the older students and had to realize that they would have to get along with others. It was in this environment that Jim learned his number one rule for being handicapped: "Pity for yourself is the worst handicap you can have."

He told me a story once of a new student who joined the school in the fourth or fifth grade after he lost his eyesight to an accident involving a blasting cap. When the new student joined the group, he was looking for sympathy for his loss. He didn't find any there since everyone else had been blind much longer and had come to grips with the fact that they would never see. What he did get was ridicule. It was harsh, but it didn't take long for the new student to realize that his pity was only getting in the way of his progress toward the rest of his life. Jim did not like having to treat the boy that way, but knew that it was the best thing for the new student to learn and this was the only way he would learn it.

During this time, Jim tried piano, but lost interest because of a personality conflict with his teacher. He learned a lot about theory of music, but never learned to read music in Braille. Later he took up the violin and played in the school orchestra.

Between his fifth and sixth grade years, Jim was invited to attend the Lion's Club Cripple Children's Camp in Kerrville, Texas. Here he learned a very valuable lesson, described in a later chapter, which he needed to live beyond his handicap and be what he wanted to be.

FRITZ AND THE BLINK: AN OVERTURE TO LIFE

Junior High School

After completing the sixth grade, the students were put into larger dorms, given freedom to roam the entire campus at will, and participate in many of the extra-curricular activities that were available. Jim was invited to join the wrestling team, which was quite an honor there. It was in the years that he was on the wrestling team that he learned his second major lesson in life: *never give up*. While Jim was not the greatest wrestler at the school, he did like to boast that he never lost a match by being pinned, though he did lose occasionally on points. He simply refused to let any opponent have the satisfaction of a win by touching both of his shoulders to the mat. That stubbornness and determination would stay with him the rest of his life, and help him become the person he would be. He also noted in his autobiography that the easiest victories came at tournaments with seeing schools, because the students evidently didn't expect the blind wrestlers to be as good as they were. I think that he kept this lesson with him all of his life, for he never underestimated his opponents, whether in verbal or physical conflict. He did, however, readily take advantage of opponents who underestimated his ability because they thought of his blindness as a handicap, as you will discover in later chapters.

— Chapter 5 —
Our Early Years

Three months each year was a short time to build a relationship with my brother. He was away at the School for the Bind nine months each year, so summers and Christmas were the two times we got to be together for extended periods of time. Summers in East Texas were warm and opportunities for mischief abounded in our little town, the woods and fields near our house, and at our grandfather's farm. We lived our summers hard and were able to pack a full year's supply of fun into every one of them.

I never knew Jim before he was blind, and he never remembered when he had sight. I never knew him when he was learning how to navigate in his dark world; I just knew he could do so with great ease. I guess I just took it for granted that all blind people could get around as well. I was never required to treat Jim with kid gloves; rather I was encouraged to treat him the same as any other brother would have been.

Jim always insisted that he was not handicapped, only inconvenienced. He asked for no favors and I didn't give any. I was always watchful for dangers he could not see and helped him avoid them, but I was careful to avoid making an issue of giving him help, just providing it when it was necessary for safety, without comment. He trusted my judgment in that regard, even though I was three years younger than he was, and I worked very hard to be worthy of that trust.

Jim helped me learn to read at a very early age with the comics in the newspaper. Once I had learned the alphabet, when I was about three years old, I would spell the words as I read and he would pronounce and define them. Being three years older, I thought that he knew everything. I would read the comics and explain the pictures and we both would laugh. Later we read comic books, and then real books.

We would play together, sleep together and fight together. Our first outdoor game was gutter ball; a game Jim played at the School for the Blind. I would roll a large ball toward him and he would listen to it rolling and hit it with a bat. On one unfortunate occasion, one of our puppies chased after the ball. Jim swung at the ball but hit the puppy. The death of that little puppy was very disturbing to Jim and gutter ball lost its appeal.

I didn't know any other blind boy games, so we just had to adapt my games to his abilities. He learned to pitch a baseball up and hit it. It took a little while to get the timing right, but he soon mastered it and I got a lot of fielding experience, catching or more often chasing the ball. I would throw it back toward him as near as possible and he would search it out with directions that I yelled from the field. Then he would hit it again. A couple of times I tried pitching the ball to him and yelling "Swing" when he should, but my pitching was so erratic that it was more frustrating than fun and we soon tired of that.

We loved to kick and pass footballs, and spent many hours every summer playing set back and passing in the open field across the street from our house. I actually became a pretty fair pass catcher, since I had to learn to adjust to the ball's flight so often. He could throw the ball a country mile, and his accuracy was pretty good, too.

I Took a Licking and Kept On Ticking

I don't really know why, but Jim and I were always fighting, not very often because we were angry, but just because we were brothers and together so much of the time. We didn't fight with fists, but rather wrestled and tussled, often on the San Augustine grass in our yard, which produced tiny scratches on our skin that would itch like crazy until we could take a good soaking bath together in the tub where we would scrub each other's backs. Wrestling was a full contact sport and sight gave me no real advantage, but Jim's size and age gave him a big edge. More often than not the bouts would end with me crying from being twisted in knots or embarrassed because Jim would hold me down and tickle me until I lost control and wet my pants.

A Little Distance Please

Out of frustration of being the continual loser, I searched for new means of fighting, which would at least provide some equality in the outcome and less pain for me. I needed some form of warfare that could provide a little distance between Jim and me so that his superior size and strength could be negated. Pea shooters, plastic straws with a diameter the size of a dried English pea, which was used as ammunition, provided such a method of warfare. Battles took place at a distance and the pain of being hit by a flying pea was much more tolerable than having your arm twisted behind your back or your guts squeezed in a leg scissors. We would square off about twenty feet apart, protected by a chair, table, or box. Armed with a straw and a box of peas we would battle for hours, only occasionally calling a truce to recover our ammunition that was all over the floor.

Rubber band guns were the next logical weapon for our combat. They were simple to make and shoot, and the danger of being shot in the eye by a hard pea was eliminated. Dad made our guns for us from scrap wood and clothes pins. We had pistols, rifles and even double-barreled versions. Dad worked at the post office, and rubber bands were plentiful and varied in sizes.

Rubber bands themselves made acceptable weapons. Looped over the thumb and index finger to make a crude crossbow, using paper rolled and folded onto a V, we could shoot back and forth at each other from the safety of our "forts" reusing the ammunition that landed around us. Those paper projectiles produced a sharp sting when they hit bare skin, and a fight generally ended with our faces, chests and arms looking like we had the chicken pox.

FRITZ AND THE BLINK: AN OVERTURE TO LIFE

It was about the same time that we had adopted this means of warfare that some genius in the dairy industry decided that milk, delivered in glass bottles at that time, could be more economically delivered in cardboard cartons that had been coated with paraffin. I hated those milk cartons because they never perfected the coating process and little chunks of wax were always breaking off and floating in your glass of milk. Not only was it a boon for the milk industry, but it supplied us with the perfect source of ammunition for our rubber band wars. The cartons could be cut into strips that then could be folded to make perfect projectiles for shooting with a rubber band. Heavier and denser than paper, they would carry farther and hit harder. The floors were often strewn with these "bullets" as Jim and I would chase each other from room to room battling each other all over the house and out into the yard.

Learning to Play Together

Later when the need to fight each other became less important than playing together, we graduated to bows and arrows for target practice only. I would make targets from cardboard boxes and tie a tin can containing a few rocks in it to the back side with a string attached to the can so I could pull on it and make rattling sounds that Jim could hear and use as a point of aim. Robin Hood and William Tell let fly many arrows in the backyard shooting at these targets.

In the large open field next to our house, we experimented with distance shooting, which accounted for the loss of many arrows in the thick grass that grew there. We also shot for altitude, shooting the arrow straight up and counting off the time it took to return to earth, then calculating the height we had achieved. It was much easier to find the arrows since they stuck straight up in the ground and usually fairly near to us. We never really worried about the arrow hitting us, though we did have a few near misses.

JOHN R. COHAGEN

Our Weapons Improve

Our grandfather had a farm out at New London, complete with barn, well house, horse (actually a mule), plowed fields, and woods. We often stayed out there and played on the eighty-five or so acres it occupied. The woods had a little stream and many good climbing trees.

One day Papaw, as we called him, introduced us to the "Nigger Shooter." (I apologize for this term, but it was the '50s, and in East Texas, that is what it was called, even by my black friends). Many people mistakenly called these weapons slingshots, but as you will see later, the slingshot was an altogether different weapon. It wasn't until many years later that I would learn that these weapons were also known as "Bean Flips." The weapon consisted of a Y-shaped handle that was hand carved from the fork of a small tree limb with rubber strips cut from an old inner tube tied to the upper ends of the Y. The two ends of the inner tube strips were tied to a leather pocket or pouch (usually cut from an old work boot). Into the pouch was placed the item to be shot. We could shoot rocks, marbles, steel ball bearings, June bugs, or about any other solid object (animal, mineral or vegetable) that would fit in the leather pouch for a distance of up to two hundred feet. Further refinements, like using surgical rubber tubing from the Army surplus store instead of inner tube strips increased our range to well over one hundred yards. A three-eighths inch ball bearing could penetrate tin barn siding or even three-quarter inch pine boards.

Cans, bottles, trees, and even cows (on rare occasions) became targets. Papaw quickly put a nix on the cows. Later, we discovered these weapons were also great for propelling large fireworks high into the sky or at the abodes of our neighbors, but that is another story.

David and Goliath

After we had perfected the use of that weapon, Papaw introduced us to another, even more powerful force, the SLINGSHOT. The Bible describes this weapon in the battle of David and Goliath as a sling. Simply, it is a leather pouch (in our case the tongue of a worn-out work boot) attached to two long thongs (trotline cord served the purpose). A loop was made in the end of one thong (this went around the middle finger) and a large knot was tied in the end of the other (to be held between the thumb and index finger). A rock was placed in the pouch, and then the slingshot was swung rapidly around the head to build up momentum. The knotted end of the cord was released as the arc of the sling approached the direction of the intended target and the rock flew out of the sling with great power and speed toward the target.

Ammunition was no problem since Granddad's farm was full of iron ore rocks. Suitable targets were a little difficult to find. Because of the range, up to two hundred yards, the targets needed to be relatively large. The house was out of the question, so was the well house. How about cars? Not on your life! Trees made good sounds as the rock would tear through the leaves and small branches, but they were no challenge. We finally decided that the tin barn should be the target of choice, range about one hundred yards. A direct hit created a marvelously loud noise, the size was right, and no one seemed to mind. We moved many pounds of rocks from the backyard driveway to the barn by this method and many dents were created in the corrugated tin that covered the walls and roof. I would shoot first. If I successfully hit the barn, Jim would line up on the sound, take aim, and let loose. His accuracy was amazing. Radar had nothing on my brother's ears.

Goliath and David

One day we did one of our truly stupid things. In front of Papaw's house there was a small boulder of iron ore. I do not know if it had been put there for decoration, or left there because it was too large to move, but it was there. It was large enough to hide behind, so I took up a position behind it from whence I could yell, giving Jim an aiming point. He would load up his slingshot, I would yell at him, and as he began his wind-up I would duck down behind the rock and wait for the sound of the fluttering rock to go over my head. It was great! There is nothing in the world like the sound of an irregularly shaped rock, flying through the air at about ninety miles per hour, spinning, fluttering and swooshing. Yell, Duck, Listen, Swoosh. Yell, Duck, Listen, Swoosh. It was a fabulous game! Yell, Duck, Listen, Swoosh. Yell, Duck, Listen, Listen, Listen. No Swoosh! I waited for a while then I stood up to see what was happening. Big mistake! I was greeted by a large rock that struck me dead center in the solar plexus! (I use the phrase *dead* center reluctantly.) THUD!

I hit the ground like a sack of potatoes. I couldn't breath. I was in severe pain. I know I was lucky that the rock didn't hit me in the head for if it had I wouldn't be writing this story today. I fully understand how Goliath could have been slain by one smooth, round, river rock, but in my case, Goliath had the sling. After 30 minutes of gasping, wheezing and crying, Little David finally got his breath back. For weeks I carried a bruise the size of a saucer on my chest and for years I had a tender spot in my chest.

Jim had dropped his original rock and had to feel around to find another. He did not let me know and I couldn't see what was going on from behind the rock. He fired his second shot without me even giving him a new aiming point but still threw the rock accurately in the direction he had originally taken aim.

I learned a valuable lesson that day and from that time on we chose our targets differently. Unfortunately, one good lesson doesn't cure all of childhood's stupidity.

FRITZ AND THE BLINK: AN OVERTURE TO LIFE

Two Little Indians

One day, just to pass the time, we were taking target practice in the backyard with our bows and arrows. I would shoot a box that we were using as the target; Jim would follow the sound of my thud and let loose an arrow in that direction. After all the shafts had flown, I would run to the target, retrieve all the arrows and we would shoot some more.

I soon decided that instead of carrying the arrows back, I would shoot them back. I mean, after all, I could see what I was doing. I would shoot them back near Jim's feet and he would gather them up. I seemed like a good plan until with one arrow I drew the bow back a little too far, and instead of landing at his feet the arrow bounced off the bone on the side of his eye socket. One inch farther to the right, and the arrow would have penetrated directly into the empty socket, and I would not have had any more stories to tell. He was more upset than hurt, but our parents insisted we not play that game any more.

The Sand Dunes

On one of our earlier vacations the family went to West Texas. One of our stops was at the Sand Dunes outside Monahans. In the midst of vast ocean of sand and scrub oak that is West Texas, you will find an area where over the centuries the winds have deposited sand creating dunes, which rise thirty or more feet above the otherwise flat terrain. It is a marvelous tourist attraction. Before the advent of dune buggies and ATVs, the only access to most of that area was by foot, or an occasional jeep. Indians had once occupied the area and a favorite pastime for the visitors was searching for arrowheads and spear points left behind centuries before and exposed from time to time by the movement of the shifting sand. I was only about five and Jim was eight when we were there, which made the height of the dunes even more impressive. We could walk in the sand, climb the dunes then slide or tumble down them with laughter and shouts of glee.

Dad wanted to help Jim appreciate the dunes more, so after a climb up a rather gentle slope to the top of one fairly tall sand dune with a flat area on top, Dad told Jim to take off running. Jim was very trusting and besides running was one of his favorite things. Dad pointed Jim in the right direction and Jim took off like a flash running across the sand and right off the edge of the drift and fell about six feet before landing in the soft sloping sand at the bottom of the steep slope. Now to you or me the thought of running blindfolded off a cliff might be frightening, but for Jim it was an exhilarating experience, one that he repeated several times before the day was over.

Run for Your Life

Not all of our time was spent playing with weapons or fighting each other. We could get ourselves into unusual situations without really trying. Like the time we were visiting Grandpa Rogers in Wichita Falls. For two kids from a small town of two thousand, this was the BIG CITY! Grandpa Rogers lived on 29th street. Heck, we didn't have twenty-nine streets in our whole town. We decided to go exploring the area around the house for several blocks. We took off walking, one of our favorite activities, next to exploring. We were on the next street over, maybe three blocks away from the house as we walked by a large brick home with a full-grown German Shepherd sitting on the front porch. As we neared the sidewalk leading to the front of the house the dog began barking. When we reached the sidewalk leading to the porch, the critter began to bear his teeth and eased down the steps to the sidewalk. To an eight-year-old, a full-grown German shepherd represents a formidable threat, but for Jim's sake I was going to stay calm and in control. As the dog increased speed in our direction, I told Jim, "The dog won't bite us if we show him we aren't scared." We stopped walking and turned to face the beast to show him we had confidence and did not fear him. Evidently, the dog had not learned that lesson. He never missed a step, coming ever closer to us, barking and baring his teeth. Then he began running straight toward us.

"RUN!" I cried, twirling Jim around to aim him down the sidewalk. Once we were up to speed, I let go of his arm, so we could both run faster. I was depending on his radar ears to be able to follow my loud footsteps as we ran for our lives. I didn't have to tell Jim twice, he took off running right beside me. However, that day his radar ears must have had something jamming them. As he ran with me, the dog nipping at our heels, he veered slightly to the left where he made the acquaintance of the trunk of a relatively large red bud tree. He couldn't have hit any more dead center, face first, one of his outstretched arms on each side. He bounced off the tree, falling flat on his back, almost on top of the charging canine. The poor animal was startled half out of his mind. He let out a yelp, tucked his tail between his legs and ran whimpering all the way back to the porch. There he sat quietly and watched us regain our composure.

I went back to Jim. He had a few small cuts on his face from the bark of the tree, but at least he was semi-conscious and very vocal. "Are you O.K.," I asked, fearing the worst.

He groaned, recovered his breath, and said sarcastically, "He won't bite if we show him we aren't scared!" Then he chuckled, got up, dusted himself off, and we continued our walk, laughing about the experience and reliving the excitement while I kept one eye peeled for any other dogs.

Life Really Swings

When I was very young, Dad decided that our yard needed to be fenced in. I don't know if this was to keep other kids and animals out or to corral Jim and me in. Dad bartered with a friend who was a welder to construct our fence. This was no simple fence, but a chain link fence with posts and top rails of four-inch diameter oil field tubing salvaged from oil wells in our area. The fence they designed would have been a proud accomplishment for Tim "the Tool Man" Taylor. That fence could have withstood a charging herd of rhinos.

Being only five years old and not familiar with the process of welding, I was curious how the pipes were "burned" together. My curiosity required that I examine one of the fresh welds. It never occurred to me that it took so long for red-hot metal to cool down. Let me just say that it doesn't take long to feel the texture of a fresh weld, but it does take a while to grow back your fingerprints.

At the finish of the job, there was sufficient pipe left to create a swing set, which was done. The swing set was engineered to the same quality as the fence. If one of those charging rhinos ever gotten over the fence, he could have safely swung on that swing set. The top bar that supported the swings was about twelve feet high and wide enough to hold two swings, one porch swing, and a trapeze. These items became a source of many hours of entertainment for two young thrill-seekers.

Jim and I loved to swing. The motion was exhilarating. As we grew older, the thrill of swinging to the limits of the swing became the goal. Swinging higher, ever higher, until the top of our arc passed the height of the frame and the chain would go slack. Then we could momentarily free-fall until the chain caught us and snatched us sharply back into reality. This was the epitome of the art of swinging and was exciting beyond words. It was an art form that only the bravest or dumbest would perform.

Jim learned that pulling the chains together just as he reached the top of the swing would pull him backward toward the top bar and increase the length of time he could free-fall. It also increased the intensity of the jerk as the chain stopped his fall. Even a steel chain will fatigue with time as Jim found out one fateful day when the chain snapped and he continued his free-fall an extra six feet or so and landed with a resounding thud, flat on his back. I figured he was dead, but eventually he moaned and began gasping for the breath, which had been knocked out of him. It took quite a while before he got his breath back, but once the chain was repaired, Jim got back on that horse without hesitation and continued to tempt fate for many years.

Falling accidentally from a swing, would be enough to discourage most people, but not Jim. We also enjoyed the sport of "bailing out," that is we intentionally jumped out of the swing to see how far we could "fly." This was scary enough for me; I could see the ground coming and prepare for the landing. I never tried it blind folded and cannot imagine what it must have felt like, from Jim's viewpoint, to jump from a swing from ten feet in the air, having to anticipate the landing on the ground that was rushing up to meet you. But Jim loved it, and as pre-teens we spent many, many hours perfecting our landings and setting new "world distance records" for bailing out of a swing. We did suffer many sprained ankles and bruises, but we never broke any bones.

Another game we often played required that we both man a swing and swing as hard as we could. When we were both at our highest swing, we would stop pumping and allow the swing to begin slowing down until it stopped, or as we called it, "let the cat die."

The frame of that swing set still stands in the yard, a reminder of those fun times, though now it is used as a trellis for jasmine to grow on. The only swing that hangs there is an "old fogy" porch swing. Often at night, before going to bed, I will go out to the swing where I am joined by my black tom cat, *King Kitty*. He will sit beside me as I push the swing with my feet to get it to a comfortable height. While the cool night air rushes past my face, I often reminisce of the years gone by when the swing set was the sight of much fun and competition. I look to my right at the houses that now stand in a subdivision where in my youth there were only trees and oil wells.

Soon I stop pumping and the swing begins to slow. When "the cat dies," King Kitty and I know it is time to go in for the night.

Tied in Knots

There weren't many sports for the blind back then, but interestingly one that was very adaptable was wrestling. It began with a fixed position with the participants in contact with one another and required pretty much continuous contact during the contest. The School for the Blind had a wrestling program and Jim was on the team for four years. He was strong as an ox and compactly built: two attributes that lend themselves to wrestling. He was also extremely agile, sometimes sitting on the floor and putting both his feet behind his head. When he would come home, I often found myself in the role of wrestling dummy. I was used to practice and perfect his holds and throws. This, however, was not my idea of fun since Jim outweighed me considerably and I was not nearly as strong as he was. This complaint remained a point of no concern to Jim. I regularly found myself being twisted and mangled by the big ox in his effort to become better at his sport. I figured I needed to find something better to occupy our time together. At least something we both could enjoy.

The Dummy Fights Back

Somewhere during this same time, I don't remember from where, we obtained a paperback book entitled *American Combat Judo*. I decided if I was going to get beat up, I might as well learn a few tricks of my own. The results were very little different. I still ended up on the short end of the stick because of our difference in size. I became very tired of bruises and strains, so I developed a strategy of self-defense of my own. One of the premier points of self-defense that the book taught was how a smaller person can control a larger person if they learn to use the physical momentum of their opponent against them and to take advantage of objects at hand as weapons of opportunity. So when the judo or wrestling got a little severe, I would run away, knowing that my opponent, in his desire to inflict pain on me, would pursue. This created the physical momentum I needed to work with. A chair moved out of its normal positions or a door pulled half shut were my weapons of choice. Was it effective? YES! Was it cruel? Well, that depends on your point of view. Cruel was what happened to me if I could not stay out of his reach until he calmed down. Does "pretzel" bring a picture to mind?

There was one good thing about this episode in my life. Because Jim was known to be a wrestler and knew Judo, everyone believed I had the same skills. I can say that this had at least some interesting effects. I never got into a fight in my entire school years because my friends *thought* I knew how to fight. As in poker, a bluff is as good as a great hand, if it works.

Vacations

For as far back as I can remember, every summer Dad would load the family in the car and head out on a two-week vacation, reminiscent of the Griswold family, in *National Lampoon's Vacation* movies. Dad had old Army buddies all over the United States and we had relatives scattered around widely, too. Dad had a goal of visiting all of the forty-eight continental states with his kids; Alaska and Hawaii were out of reach. By the time I was twelve, I had been in all forty-eight contiguous states, Canada and Mexico. Though I do not remember a lot about all the places I have been because we started this when I was so young, I thank Dad for completing his goal. It gives me a sense of pride as an American to be able to say I have seen it all.

Our trips were always adventures that consisted of long hours of riding in the back seat while eating pork n' beans and Vienna sausages and playing games. To this day, I cannot stand the thought of eating another Vienna sausage. We carried a small ice chest filled with drinks and snacks. We only stopped when we needed gas or saw some interesting spot that deserved closer inspection.

Back then, Cokes came in 6-1/2 oz green bottles and had the name of the town and state where they were first filled embossed on the bottom. We would start collecting these bottles on the day we left on the trip to try to see how many different states we could collect before we got home. Duplicates were used to recover the penny deposit when we stopped for gas and bought a new supply of drinks. Some of the duplicates never made it back to the store, however, since they were used as traveling latrines. Jim and I would fill them up and toss them out the window to avoid having to make any more pit stops than were absolutely necessary.

[Don't try Passing]

[On A Slope]

[Unless You Have]

[A Periscope]

[Burma Shave]

I still remember looking for those little red and white signs that occasionally would be spotted on the side of the roadways. Burma Shave had created an ad campaign using these signs with their catchy nonsensical poems to sell their shaving cream, but in doing so they provided occasional entertainment in otherwise long hours of riding. We would relish their every word, repeating them over and over again.

Nights Were Interesting, Too!

Our day's drive would often end at either a friend's or a relative's house where we would eat, sleep and prepare for the next day. Other days we would stop at the cheapest motel we could find, or on one trip we carried a tent for the nights we weren't staying with someone. I still have memories of one hotel we stayed in near Kansas City, Kansas. We stayed on the second floor and there was only one bathroom at the end of the hall to serve all the rooms on that floor.

We also had to go through the capital of ever state we entered, so Dad could get a picture of the capitol building, usually with Mom, Jim and me sitting on the steps to the front entrance.

We saw it all. We experienced everything. We walked down into Grand Canyon, visited Meteor Crater, the Petrified Forest, and Disneyland only the second year it was open. We went to Walla Walla, Washington, Hoover Dam, Glacier National Park in Canada,

FRITZ AND THE BLINK: AN OVERTURE TO LIFE

Yellowstone Park, Luray Caverns in Kentucky, Hershey Park in Pennsylvania, New York City (where Jim got Mickey Mantle's autograph), Green Bay, Wisconsin, Washington, D.C. (we climbed the George Washington Monument), the Covered Bridges of New Hampshire, Philadelphia (we touched the Liberty Bell), Miami, New Orleans (the French Quarter). But no matter where we went, it was so good to get home.

These trips gave Jim and me a chance to see that the entire world is not like home, but anywhere could be home, and that people were friendly everywhere, even in Yankee territory. We discovered that the whole world is not like East Texas, that Laird Hill was not the tallest mountain around, and there were actually cities bigger than Dallas. We got to see where cotton was grown, as well as corn, wheat, and lumber. We saw dairy farms, cattle ranches, and where Hershey's chocolate was made. We saw it all! Other kids in our town had seen Disney Land on television, but we had been there, ridden the rides and talked to Mickey Mouse. We had been to the top of the Statue of Liberty, the Washington Monument and Pike's Peak. We had a perspective of life that few in our school could share. It was the greatest gift our parents could give us.

— Chapter 6 —
Getting a Bang Out of Life

There is something special about sound to a blind man. We've all heard that when you lose one of our senses, the others sharpen to compensate for that loss. I guess that is the way it was with Jim. His hearing was incredible, his balance superb. He could echo locate by snapping his fingers and listening to the echoes from objects about him. He could hear you breathing across the room. He could identify a person approaching by the sound of their footsteps; even by the way they breathed.

As color stimulates the seeing, sound stimulated Jim. He loved music. He learned to play the violin, guitar, mandolin, banjo, and harmonica. His favorite was the classical guitar. Chet Atkins was his idol in the music world. Strong sounds, loud sounds, and music energized him. For a blind person sounds create a picture, tones create the color, but noise creates the sensation of power.

I was no good at music, but from a very early age, I learned to love fireworks and Jim loved them, too. Fireworks in those days were relatively cheap, and Dad discovered that if they were bought in bulk at wholesale distributors, they were even cheaper.

Reader Warning

If you do not really enjoy fireworks or find them distasteful, then this chapter is not for you, but it was a very big part of our childhood. I do tend to get a little wordy and technical in my descriptions of our antics and inventions, but if you loved fireworks when you were young as much as we did, you will appreciate the details of our ingenious modifications. Either way, this chapter reveals a lot about the workings of our minds.

FRITZ AND THE BLINK: AN OVERTURE TO LIFE

It All Started with Santa Clause

Every Christmas, hidden under the tree and in our stockings hung on our fake fireplace, but never gift-wrapped, we could depend on finding three or four large cardboard cartons filled with an infinite variety of noisemakers, sparklers, cones, and rockets. We never had much use for cones; they just sat there and burned, spewing out sparks and pretty colors, but no racket. Roman candles were neat. We could use them like cannons shooting tracer rounds. Sparklers were virtually useless, except when used as time-delay fuses for other fireworks. Otherwise, they were simply something to burn your fingers on.

Buzz Bombs, Rockets, Repeating Star shells (especially those containing the loud salutes) were among our favorites because they flew in the air, they made noise, in the proper hands they could be aimed, and they were easily modified. Fire crackers ranged from the tiny ladyfingers, to regular firecrackers, to Baby Giants, Silver Bombs, and Cherry Bombs. The last three were especially popular because they had waterproof fuses and went BOOM instead of bang. The silver bomb was our first choice, because it could be easily modified, with only a pocket knife and airplane cement, to hold the powder from six silver bombs in one casing. Now that was a firecracker! We saved the empty casings and filled them with powder taken from smaller firecrackers at a later time. We even ordered waterproof fuse, advertised in the back of comic books in those days, in fifty foot coils so we could extend the time delay on the fireworks, link them together or simply build our own.

With this kind of arsenal, a little imagination and a lot of boredom (generated by living in a small town), Jim and I developed many new and useful pyrotechnic creations.

JOHN R. COHAGEN

Our Early Experiments

No firework was ever created for the intentions Jim and I had in mind. Simply making noise was fun, but more noise would be better. Throwing fireworks was fun, junior grenades, but propelling them mechanically, via slingshot, bean flip, catapult, or bow and arrow was a vast improvement. The later development of methods to propel one firecracker using a tube and a smaller firecracker or even a rocket to send the main charge higher expanded our noisemaking universe to untold heights.

We discovered that tape could be used to hold fireworks to the point of an arrow. Jim would draw the bow back, arrow in notch, as I would light the fuse and yell "fire." A firecracker that was carried aloft in this manner could be heard much better, and farther, if it exploded in the air, instead of on the ground. Shoot, we may have been the inventors of the first Inter-Continental Ballistic Arrow.

Across the street from our house lived a very nice, older lady, Mrs. Nixon, our local Avon representative. She was on occasion our babysitter when the folks had to go out of town. I don't know why it was, but Jim and I enjoyed irritating her. One evening, we were in the front yard enjoying our fireworks, small stuff, just bangs. Mrs. Nixon phoned over to the house and told Dad that we were disturbing her. Could we, please, go to the backyard to pop our fireworks?

Dad came outside and informed us that we needed to move to the back, so we would not disturb Mrs. Nixon. Being obedient, though mischievous, we readily complied.

The backyard was O.K. for a while, but most of the things we could pop fireworks in or at had been previously used and represented little challenge to the active mind of youth. The very idea that we had been evicted from our own front yard created a challenge that had to be addressed. Think! Plan! Scheme! We had at our disposal dozens and dozens of bottle rockets. But the problem was they went too high and weren't loud enough to be useful as an effective irritant or bombardment weapon. Perhaps adding a little weight would lower the trajectory so that they would fall to earth before exploding. Sure, and if that weight happened to be a firecracker, all the better. And if the firecracker could be delayed from exploding until it had fallen back near to the ground or on it, success would be ours.

A little sewing thread or masking tape would solve the attachment problem. The bottle rocket had a report built into it, but it was not near loud enough and besides, it exploded as soon as the rocket burned out of propellant, too high to be an effective nuisance. That was easily solved. We pulled off the head of the rocket and removed the flash powder.

Delaying the explosion was the big problem. If we lit the fuse on the firecracker and then the rocket, the firecracker might blow up too soon, even before the rocket left the ground, certainly before it reached Mrs. Nixon's front yard. After all, we had to propel our attack weapon over the house. If we twisted the fuses together and lit the rocket fuse it could delay the firecracker burst, we tried, but still not enough delay. The firecracker rarely passed the apex of our roof before the firecracker exploded.

Finally, by a stroke of genius, we arrived at the solution. We taped the firecracker high on the rocket so the tip of the fuse reached only slightly below the nozzle. We tied the fuse to the stick of the rocket so that the tip of the fuse would not be lit until the firing rocket emitted sparks. The fuse then had to burn all the way to the firecracker before it would explode while the rocket was carrying it toward its target. Eureka!!! Rockets prepared in this manner successfully flew over the house and fell into the street and front yard of our victim before exploding. For several minutes we successfully rained terror down on our victim.

Success was sweet, but our victory was short lived. Within minutes of mounting our assault Dad received another phone call about the noise. He assured Mrs. Nixon that we were not guilty; he could see us playing in the backyard through the kitchen window. It wasn't until many years later that I finally told Dad the truth about that night. It was funny at that time, and I truly believe it would have been funny to him had he known that time. After all, as Jim well knew, Dad thought she was a pest.

JOHN R. COHAGEN

Dodge Rocket — Sport of Kings

What's the use of having radar ears if you can't use them for some practical use? Sure, walking down the street and avoiding running into cars, walls and the like is great, but what about smaller objects, like bottle rockets. Perfect! "Jim, you get at the end of the street and I will shoot bottle rockets at you. You can hear them coming and dodge them." What a delightful game! I could hold the stick of a bottle rocket in the tips of my fingers, light it, aim it with some degree of accuracy and fire it at a target up to 200 feet away or I could shoot them out of a piece of pipe like a bazooka. The probability of a hit was slight, but I could get very close on occasion. Of course, I got the better end of the deal. I shot the rockets while Jim got to dodge them. It was a sport that we enjoyed on many occasions burning up several hundred bottle rockets.

You Only Light It Once

One of our favorite aerial fireworks was the single shot salute. Based on a principle we later adopted for our own, a large firecracker, resembling a silver bomb, was mounted in a cardboard cylinder glued to a wooden base containing an lesser amount of black powder used to propel the larger charge high into the air. The resulting explosion and flash could be heard and seen for nearly a mile. Other types of shells were also available; they shot stars, multiple firecrackers, and salutes (single loud bombs) in the air. There were also multi-shot versions of these where the fuse ran through several tubes mounted to a single base. Light it and back away. The fuse burned through each tube in succession setting off multiple aerial fireworks with a delay between the shots. They came in three-shot, five-shot and ten-shot repeaters.

One night we were going to let Jim light a five-shot repeater. He set it in the middle of the street, between our yard and the Assembly of God parsonage next to Mrs. Nixon's house. He set the contraption on the ground, felt out the tip of the fuse, applied the hot end of the lighter, heard the sizzle, indication the fuse was burning, and backed quickly away, tripping on the curb and falling into the chain link fence bordering our yard.

POP! The charge went off propelling the first shell high into the air. BOOM! The report sounded clearly throughout the neighborhood. Ready for more fun, Jim jumped up and dashed into the street to light the second tube. "STOP!" we yelled. We shouted at him to back up, that it was still lit. He locked his legs and slid feet first into the repeating shell, toppling it over in the direction of the parsonage just as the second shell fired from its tube. This shell happened to be a whistling chaser. It shot directly through one pane of the livingroom window of the parsonage, ignited and began running around on the floor whistling and blowing smoke and sparks everywhere before finally exploding. We could see the flash through the window. Fortunately, or unfortunately, as was the case, Brother Bell and his family were not home. Dad ran quickly to the repeating shell and set it erect again before the last three tubes fired. Even as the display continued he had to break the window glass on the door to unlock it and get into the livingroom to see that no fire was burning.

No real damage was done other than the two broken panes of glass, which were replaced, but the story of that incident lived on for many years as a legend in our neighborhood.

Moon Rocket from Hell

Rockets were a real technological challenge. This was the late '50s and man hadn't been in space yet except in the movies. The space age was around the corner and with only limited funds and resources Jim and I were on the leading edge of Space Age Weapons Research. Fireworks of the time offered our best hope. One in particular was very promising; a two-stage rocket, complete with a pointed plastic nosecone and plastic fins. Designed to deliver a load of brightly colored stars high into the night sky, the possibilities for the delivery of larger and louder salutes provided the challenge we sought.

Getting rid of the stars was easy enough. Take off the nosecone and pour them out. Maybe they could be used in future experiments, but for now they were just waste. The next challenge was to create a new firework that would fit in the space remaining above the existing rocket motor, shaped and sized to fit neatly in the space available. At the same time we had to provide for the maximum amount of flash powder that could be lifted by the rocket. Paper napkins, masking tape, and the powder from sixty firecrackers seem to be just the ticket. A couple of hours of diligent work at the breakfast table were needed to empty the firecrackers of their precious dust, roll a thick-walled cylinder, and pack it with powder. Then we had to install a couple of fuses and seal the entire thing with masking tape until the proper size and shape were attained to fit snugly in the rocket.

With great anticipation we carried the rocket to the street in front of the house, set it on its white plastic fins, nose pointed to the sky, lit the fuse and waited for the successful detonation of the largest and highest explosion we had ever produced. With a loud swoosh the first stage ignited carrying the rocket skyward. It flew straight and true to an altitude of about two hundred and fifty feet. There was a pause between stages when the rocket was supposed to slow and turn approximately ninety degrees to streak across the sky before dispersing the beautiful stars.

We did make one slight miscalculation. Because we wanted the maximum explosion possible, we did not consider the effects of the weight of the salute. The extra weight caused the nose of the rocket passed horizontal and when the second stage fired it pushed the rocket earthward instead of across the sky. Where would it go? What would it hit? The trajectory, luckily, targeted a large pasture. Only feet above the ground the salute fired, or more accurately, spewed with a large white flame, directed downward by the cylinder that enclosed it. No Boom!

It was late summer and the grass in the pasture was tall and dry, easily ignited by the hurtling flame-thrower we had created. It was night so the flames were easy to see, even from my vantage point two blocks away. This had been a private, invitation only launch, and no one else was around, so Jim and I ran arm in arm to the scene, instantly transforming from space scientists to forest ranger fire fighters. Down the street we ran. We climbed through the barbed wire fence and ran to the small fire that we had started. Stomping like Italian wine makers, we were able to subdue the fire before it could burn off more than about a ten-foot circle. Since there had been no great boom to announce the "success" of our efforts, none of the neighbors were aroused to witness our failure. We returned home quietly under the cover of darkness, sooty but wiser, and determined that we would repeat the flight someday.

UFOs — R-US

Our house was built before the days of central air conditioning and heating. We were cooled by evaporating fans and attic fans and heated by floor furnaces and space heaters. You've never lived until you have stepped barefooted on the grid covering a hot floor furnace and had blisters in the form of a checkerboard burned onto the soles of your feet. But I digress.

The '60s brought on the age of plastics. More and more everyday items were being made from plastics. Boxes, milk containers, (thank goodness, I hated drinking wax chips) and bottles of all shapes and sizes. The most wonderful of all was the filmy plastic bag used to cover freshly laundered clothes at the dry cleaners. It was marvelous, just right for our purposes. It was lightweight, airtight, and easily obtained. A little thread to tie off the ends and you had the perfect bag for a lighter-than-air balloon. All that was lacking was a lighter-than-air gas to fill the bag with. The government regulated helium, so it was not readily available and was expensive. These two facts forced us to seek another source. It was a minor setback to two budding geniuses. Methane would serve the purpose. It was lighter than air and readily available from any number of spare gas jets installed in the house. There were a few drawbacks. The methane would not produce the lift of either helium or hydrogen used in blimps or rigid airships (like the ill-fated Hindenburg) and like hydrogen, methane was flammable, but then that proved to be a plus.

Construction soon began on a number of gas-filled balloons to which we attached messages and sent aloft. Strangely, we only got one reply from a farmer north of Texarkana, Arkansas, about one hundred and fifty miles away. Maybe there was a better use for our balloons than delivering messages. Of course! They could carry our fireworks higher into the sky. Quick experimentation soon proved that a full bag could easily carry the weight of an overfilled silver bomb with four feet of cannon fuse higher than any method we had previously employed.

One fateful night we unleashed our newest creation on the world. The sun was down, the air was cooling, and the moonless sky was dark. The launch was made and the clear bag floated majestically and silently disappeared in the starry heavens. The only evidence of its existence was an occasional shower of sparks from the fuse as pieces of it burned away and fell from the sky. Higher and higher it went. We really didn't know how long it took to burn four feet of fuse. I guess it really didn't matter too much, since the balloon was already higher than anything we had ever sent up with fireworks in the past.

Eventually it happened. A bright white flash lit up the sky followed a couple of seconds later by a resounding BOOM that echoed for thirty seconds off the hills and houses around us. The explosion blew the bag open and ignited the methane gas. The fire created a magnificent blue and yellow boiling flame in the sky, a sight that could not be missed by the several sets of eyes whose ears had heard the explosion and looked up to find its source. Rapidly the gas and plastic were consumed and once again the sky was dark except for the beautiful stars in the moonless summer sky. Jim and I retired for the night, joyful with our successful first flight of our airbag bomb.

The next day the town was full of talk and rumors. There were UFO sightings, meteor reports, even a report that a plane had exploded over our little town according to some. No evidence was ever found to substantiate any of those claims, and Jim and I never offered our explanation. It is more interesting sometimes for people to believe what they want than to know the truth.

It's No Surprise If It Whistles

In those days of limitless pyrotechnic opportunities, there was available to the prankster a device known as an "Auto Fooler," a whistling chaser with report that had an electrical igniter with wires that could be attached to the sparkplugs of a car. When the car was started, the spark from the plug ignited the chaser creating a loud and long whistle, accompanied by smoke, and followed by a resounding bang. Many an unsuspecting victim succumbed to this fate. So often, in fact, that it became quite a routine occurrence. It was no great surprise, only a nuisance since after the attack, the victim had to lift the hood and remove the wires that ignited the device, so the car would run smoothly because the wires shorted out the spark plugs to which they had been attached. Surely, with a little effort a more surprising variation could be produced.

Faced with this new challenge, Jim and I decided that the whistle had to go and the bang, greatly increased in strength to a BOOM, should be a total surprise, not an announced upcoming event. To that end, we dismantled an "Auto Fooler" and retrieved the electrical igniter, then reinstalled it into a silver bomb that had been enhanced with a larger powder charge, of course. We extended the wires with bell wire so that the bomb could lie on the ground, avoiding damage to the engine. Voila! Now we needed a victim to test the effectiveness of our new design.

Victims were readily available to us. Our parents often had bridge club parties at our home. Tonight was such a night. We quickly, but carefully, chose our prey from the guest list; someone with a sense of humor and known to have interesting reactions to surprises in the past. Our victim was "Mickey" Butts. With a name like Butts you had to have a sense of humor, and we knew he could take a joke since he had been the target of many practical jokes by our dad.

Under cover of darkness, with the distraction of the bridge game, we climbed under the car and set our newly developed device in place. The bridge parties had a way of lasting long into the night, and patience was not one of our virtues, we were always too busy coming up with new ideas to simply sit and wait. Unfortunately, or luckily, we were not at the house when the party broke up and "Mickey" and his wife Pat, Pat Butts, left the party. I swear that was her name. "Mickey" always joked about his Aunt Ophelia Butts.

We later learned that the bomb had functioned perfectly, taking the victims completely and totally by surprise. So much so, that Mickey took several silent minutes of sitting in his car, white as a sheet, to recover his composure before attempting to drive home. He told us later that he was really shaken by the incident at the time, but he was able to look back on it, after some time had passed, as a great "Gotcha!"

The Night the Town Blew Up

Our ultimate noisemaker was the product of boredom more than design. One evening as we sat around the house with nothing particular to do, we began breaking open firecrackers and emptying the powder onto a paper towel. We had no particular plan at the time and were just building up a supply of flash powder for future use. We sat there talking, joking, and emptying powder until we had emptied maybe one hundred and twenty firecrackers. Our fingers were sore, so we decided that was enough. The flash powder we had collected would fill a small pill bottle. This would have been great for re-stuffing many silver bombs to capacity, but by this time they had been outlawed and we had long since shot up the last of our supply of empty casings.

We could have made eight to ten pretty fair-sized bombs from that much powder, but it seemed like such a waste of effort to make small bombs when we had the capability to make one huge firecracker, Texas size with a capital T. So we took the easy path and made a single bomb that grew to the size of a softball after being wrapped in several alternating layers of napkin and masking tape. We had one hundred and twenty unused fuses, which we tied and wound together with sewing thread to create a Texas sized fuse that measured about six feet in length and would give sufficient time to leave the proximity and establish the necessary alibi. We had a firecracker that would shake the town.

We intended to do no damage; only to liven things up a little on a very dull summer evening in a small East Texas town. The new post office had only recently been completed, and across the street from that sat Pope and Turner Hardware and Furniture. In the back window of that store, lighted for the world to see was the most enormous steel ball, actually a safe, which you could ever hope to see. The two buildings formed a canyon, which we believed would help direct the sound of our creation like a megaphone, increasing the effectiveness of its sound making capability.

With our masterpiece safely out of view in a Piggly Wiggly grocery bag, we left the house and walked casually the six or so blocks to the intended ground zero. Once there, we carefully laid the beauty in the middle of the street, lit the fuse and walked a little more briskly, back to Rawlinson's Grocery Store about three blocks away. We bought a couple of Dr. Peppers, at that time only ten cents apiece and sat on the front porch sipping them and waiting for the announcement that our experiment had been successful. The suspense was terrible; time passed more slowly than when you are having a tooth pulled. Finally, when we had just begun to worry that the fuse had failed, we were rewarded with the sound of an explosion the likes of which that town had not heard since the 1930s when an old oil separator blew up near the high school.

The sound was beautiful. It echoed off the buildings and trees for what seemed forever. The megaphone theory had worked. Soon after the echoes subsided, the night air began to ring with a new and different sound. Sirens! Do you know how many different types of sirens are used on police cars, sheriff's cars, highway patrol cars, and even Texas Rangers' cars? We got to hear a large range of variations that night; an unexpected symphony for Jimmy's ears and an encore to our opus.

We sat on the porch of the store for a little while longer and finished our drinks, so we wouldn't have to pay the two-cent deposit to take them with us. Then we meandered slowly back to ground zero to see what was going on. It wasn't hard to see with all the headlights, flashing red lights and spotlights the different vehicles had on them illuminating the scene with many colors, and several persons, in a variety of uniforms, looking high and low with their flashlights. There was still some smoke in the area, though most had dissipated by the time we arrived, but the unmistakable smell of flash powder hung heavy in the cool night air. In the middle of that gravel and asphalt street was a small crater, maybe twelve inches across and four inches deep, but very little else remained save a six-foot, curved line of black-stained gravel leading to the pit where the fuse had burned on the pavement.

No one ever really knew what happened that night, and it was not a topic that was greatly discussed, except in very private conversations, for many years. No one was hurt and the crater was no larger than many potholes in our city streets anyway, but from that time on, Jim and I decided that we should stick to smaller noisemakers. Shortly after that, the truly great fireworks we had grown up with were outlawed and the amount of powder allowed in standard fireworks was soon reduced so drastically that they were no longer as much fun. Our great pyrotechnic career slowly drifted into oblivion, but not before supplying us with memories of great accomplishments that would be joyful recollections for the rest of our lives.

— Chapter 7 —
Special Events That Molded Jim's Life

Because of his outgoing personality, his self-assurance, and his positive attitude about his handicap, Jim was offered many opportunities to travel. He never missed an opportunity to experience something new, and jumped at any chance to do so.

Kerrville Camp

It was 1955, Jim was ten, and summer had come to Texas. Jim had been invited to attend the Cripple Children's Camp sponsored by the Lion's Club in Kerrville, Texas. I remember it well because that summer the city poured curb and gutter in front of our house. We poured a sidewalk extension to the new curb and in that concrete Dad had me put my footprints. Jim was not there, so Dad wrote in the wet concrete, "1955 Jim at Kerrville Camp." That reminder is still there.

The camp was a two-week affair, providing cripple children and deaf children the opportunity to enjoy the camping experience. It was the first time that Jim had been away from home alone except under the supervision of the School for the Blind. Jim was the only blind child at the camp, and the first blind child invited to attend the camp since the decision to include the blind had just recently been made. There was much apprehension on the part of my parents and the counselors at the camp who had no experience with a blind camper.

Needless to say, Jim did not give this a second thought; he never seemed to have any fear of new experiences. He only anticipated trying something different. He not only had a great time, but also won the outstanding camper award for his participation in almost every activity available. He came home with a mountain of stuff he had made in the different arts and crafts; baskets, bracelets, lanyards, birdhouses, leather wallets, medals for swimming, canoeing and other various activities.

He so impressed his instructors that many of them continued to write to him for years, just to see how he was doing. Any concerns they may have had about dealing with the blind soon changed to respect for this most unusual and independent camper.

It was there, Jim claimed in his life story, that he learned the most valuable lesson about dealing with his handicap.

"*One of my most valuable friendships was with a man named Dick Vanviber, although I called him Van. Van was a veteran who was blinded during the Second World War. Since that time, he had regained some of his vision— enough that he could get around, but not enough that he could read very small print. He spent his time working with blind persons, helping them to learn to do for themselves, which he considered to be most important. The thing that I remember Van for most, however, was not something he taught me; it was something he told me.*

"*On the very last day of camp Van came over to the cabin and asked if I would come out and talk to him for a minute. Of course, I did. We went out to where there were some benches under the shade of a tree and sat down. Van talked about other things for a minute and then got straight to the point of his conversation.*

"*'Jim,' he questioned in a voice which had now become quite serious, 'what would you say the main difference between a person who can't see and a blind person is?'*

"*This is not the easiest type of question to answer, especially when it is directed at a ten-year-old boy. I told him I didn't guess I could say.*

"*'Well, then, let me tell you my ideas.' This was the most serious talking to that I can remember up until that time. We talked for a long time about many things. The main idea, though, he put this way.*

"*'Jim, the only thing that is wrong with a person who can't see is just that. A blind person, on the other hand, has far more wrong with* him, because not only can't he see with his eyes, he can't see with his mind. This is far worse than not being able to see.'"

I think this was something that Jim already believed in the back of his mind. He had never before in his life considered himself limited by his lack of sight. Having another person whom he respected articulate this point helped lock that belief in his mind and heart. It would have a profound effect on his attitude about the School for the Blind and ultimately lead to a decision that would have a great effect on the remainder of his life.

Boy Scouts

Jim was a rugged individual, never pampered, never asking special favors from anyone. At the School for the Blind, he was a member of the orchestra, playing violin; he was on the track team, wrestling team, and a member of the Boy Scouts. Jim was selected, by the Lions Club that sponsored his Boy Scout troop to be one of five scouts from that troop to go to the National Jamboree in 1958 in Valley Forge, Pennsylvania. There he gained much recognition for his ability to participate in camping and other scouting activities to the amazement of those who only saw him as a blind kid.

Jim did not go unprepared. He had been told of the opportunities that he would have to trade for souvenirs, though buying and selling was discouraged. So before leaving for the Jamboree, Jim packed away several neckerchiefs, and other scouting items that were identifiable with Texas, and Austin, but his greatest trading items were the products of his imagination.

Since everyone knew that "all Texans were oil men" and had wells in their backyards, Jim had Dad go to our papaw's farm, where there happened to be oil wells and tap off about half a gallon of Black Gold, Texas Tea, crude oil. This was then carefully dispensed into one ounce medicine bottles, capped, sealed, and appropriately labeled to maximize their value as barter items. About forty of these were in his suitcase when he left.

His other great trading item was a bag full of sweet gum balls. These were round, covered with thorny spikes, and spray painted white. Now Jim was a true southerner. He had a natural distrust, even dislike, for Yankees. He figured, and it would seem that history proved him correct, that he could pass off the painted sweet gum balls as porcupine eggs. He must have been right, because he came home with more neat items than you could possibly imagine. For me it was a fourteen-inch Samurai sword with a red tassel, a gift I prized for many years. Whether people actually believed that story about the porcupine eggs or not, he was able to trade away everyone he had. If I know Jim, it was probably done with a showmanship that would rival the great P. T. Barnum.

Fly Fishing

One of our favorite relatives when we were young was Mom's brother, Cecil. Cecil was a Naval Pilot in World War II and flew the Grumman Bear Cat off the *U.S.S. Intrepid.* He did not like to talk about his war experiences and he suffered nightmares for years after the war because of them. He was a large man, a handsome man (I thought he looked like Sterling Hayden) and a funny man, with a slow, southern drawl and humor that reminds me now of Andy Griffith. To Jim and me, he was bigger than life.

Mom loved to tell the story about when he was discharged from the Navy after the war. He was supposed to fly his plane from where his ship was docked back to the Naval Air Station in San Antonio. He took a little detour and flew up to Overton to buzz the family. Dad had a photographic studio on the second floor of one of the buildings downtown, and Mom worked there, too. When Cecil got to Overton he turned the plane up on its wing and flew down the main street just above the buildings with the engine of that warplane at full throttle. Mom swore she could see him wink at her from the cockpit.

Cecil continued to fly after the war in his private planes. He had a drilling mud company in south Louisiana and the planes provided quick and affordable transportation to his customers' drilling sites. He would often come to Overton in his plane to visit, and he would take Jim and me on flights. We always knew when he arrived; he would buzz the house or the school to let us know to come to Henderson to the airport to pick him up.

At different times in his business career, he owned sea planes, so he could land on the ocean or in rivers and lakes. In one of these, Jim and I got to go on one of our most memorable fishing trips to the Chandelier Islands, about seventy-five miles south of New Orleans in the Gulf of Mexico. We flew over the swamps of south Louisiana and saw alligators. We flew over the Gulf Coast and could see schools of fish. Over the Gulf of Mexico, we saw numerous waterspouts, tornadoes over water, and finally we came to the Chandelier Islands. In the middle of nowhere, there were several small islands, none bigger than a football field, separated by shallow, clear water.

We landed and taxied up to one of the islands, unloaded our fishing gear, waded out about waist deep and began to fish. Up until now it had all been fun. But when we started catching sharks regularly, I began to have doubts as to whether I really wanted to be a fisherman. Jim and I each caught a very respectable red snapper; the only two edible fish caught that day. The sharks we were catching were very small, no more than two feet long, but they were enough to make you keep one eye on the water around you at all times. I don't know how Jim could stand there and fish not being able to see what was swimming around him. The fishing trip ended very abruptly, however, when Cecil yelled at Jim and me to get on the pontoons of the airplane, QUICK! He and Dad headed for the beach and Jim and I scrambled onto the pontoons. A six-foot shark had swum right through Cecil's legs while he was not paying close attention. It was agreed that it was time to go home.

The flight home was uneventful, but that night we had broiled snapper with lemon and butter. We retold the story of the trip in the safety of the living room and bragged on our fish.

Canes Get in the Way

Some years later, Jim was invited to a camp in Arkansas that specialized in teaching the blind how to gain mobility and independence by using a cane. This was right up his alley. If there was anything Jim wanted, it was mobility and independence. For two weeks the instructors worked with Jim, teaching him the techniques of using the cane to locate objects, avoid collisions, etc. Family was not allowed at the camp, so for two weeks we wondered how he was progressing.

Finally came graduation day. We made a special trip to the camp to attend the graduation and bring Jim home. At the ceremony he was given his certificate and a new aluminum cane, which to this day still hangs on the wall of my shop as a reminder of my brother's free spirit. In fact, about all that cane ever did was to hang on the wall as a souvenir of the camp since Jim refused to use it because it advertised to the world, "Here comes a blind person!"

The truth of the matter was that for the two weeks Jim spent at the camp, most of his time was not learning to use a cane, but rather teaching his blind instructors how to get around without one. Once Jim had walked around an area for a few times, he could produce a map in his mind of the major features he would encounter. Fixed objects were no real problem, but smaller objects and objects that were often moved posed a greater threat. In unfamiliar surroundings, Jim would adopt a shuffling walk to feel for small objects and changes in elevation, and he snapped his fingers and listened for the echo to locate larger ones. He perfected a navigation system of his own that offered him freedom of movement without canes, dogs or other aids that would detract from his independence.

Seeing-Eye Dogs Are No Better

After the cane experience failed, Jim was offered a "Seeing Eye Dog." At the insistence of the Seeing Eye Foundation, Jim was given a tri-colored, smooth-haired Collie named Campy to live with and become accustomed to. He was a beautiful dog, white with tan and black markings, smooth short hair that shed like leaves in the fall, a long pointed snout, and a tongue that could lick your hand free of fried chicken grease in seconds. Jim loved that dog, and Campy loved Jim.

Campy ate with him, slept with him and lived with him. The dog did have two major flaws. He was terrified by fireworks, which meant he had to be sheltered from our favorite pastime, and more importantly, everything that animal ate turned to gas. Jim's room soon took on an ambiance all its own.

We kept that dog for over a year, creating the necessary bond required for training the animal to be a qualified lead dog. Before the training began, however, we received a letter from the Seeing Eye Foundation telling us that Campy was a very special animal, one of the rarest of his breed. He was the only known tri-colored, smooth-haired Collie known to be fertile and capable of producing pure white puppies, and they would like to have him back for breeding purposes.

Jim was disappointed at having to give up such a fine friend, though he did admit that he had no intentions of ever using a dog as a guide. The dog did play an important role on one occasion in protecting his master. One evening, after one of his infamous drinking outings, Jim returned home and was let out of the car by his drinking buddy at the end of the driveway. At this time, the driveway was not paved and it had developed a pretty severe hole near the end. My parents were hosting the bridge club that night and many of the guests were in the living room, which was on the front of the house near the driveway. As Jim toddled unsteadily toward the entrance to his room, he stepped in the aforementioned hole, and though he had great balance under normal circumstances, the alcohol consumption of that night made him a little less than stable on his feet. There was a resounding thud as he hit the ground, followed by a loud epithet that pierced the din of the bridge club. My dad came to the front door to find Jim sprawled out in the driveway, struggling to get to his feet.

"Jim, are you OK?" he called.

Jim replied, with a noticeable slur in his voice, "Yes, sir, I just tripped in this hole!" With that he got to his feet and carefully made his way to his room where Campy was anxious for his master to return. Still unsteady, and now slightly shaken by the fall, Jim was not ready for his excited friend to jump on his chest with both front feet, but the dog was used to being greeted in this manner and proceeded as usual. Again Jim lost his balance and fell to the floor between the door and his bed, flat on his back with the full weight of an eighty-pound dog on his chest and a nine-inch tongue joyfully licking his face in greeting.

Dad had made his way through the house from the front door and suddenly entered the other side of the room. "Are you all right, Jim?" he asked again.

"Yesh, shir," Jim slurred. "I'm just pettin' the dawg." With that Dad returned to the party.

The next morning, Jim told me that later Dad came to wake him to get ready for church. In a voice more stern than pleasant, Dad announced, "Jim, I think you had BETTER get ready for church." So far as I know the incident was never mentioned again.

Don't Drink the Water

The summer after high school, Jim got the opportunity through a student exchange program to spend six weeks in Saltillo, Mexico, living with a Mexican family and one other American student to study Spanish in a way that no classroom could afford. Jim jumped at the opportunity and soon was on his way, alone, on a flight to Mexico. There he was joined by another student from Haaavud, better known as Harvard to those who speak non-Bostonian English. In the home where they stayed, no one spoke English, even Jim and his friend were not supposed to converse in English, though they did when they were alone at night.

Together they toured the countryside, shopped, and took part in activities with the family. Jim only drank cokes and other bottled drinks, but he did eat any food the family prepared. He loved spicy foods, but sometimes they did not like him, thus leading his roommate to nickname him Eros, God of the Winds. Jim came home with a superior knowledge of the Spanish language, and a greater appreciation for the American way of life and eating.

— Chapter 8 —
The High School Years

After eight years of being taught how to be a blind person, Jim, now a teenager decided it was time he left the School for the Blind to attend public school. It was not so much that the school did not provide a fine education, but rather their curriculum, in his mind, was geared toward teaching blind students how to become blind people. He recalls in his autobiography, *"I didn't like being told that blind persons shouldn't go to college, and therefore, the school would not provide a more adequate program in sciences and math."* Even at the young age of 13, this went against every vision Jim had for his future. He realized that the school was teaching him to be limited by his blindness, and his vision of the future had no limitations. His discontent grew through the year, and by the end of the year, Jim had made up his mind that he would not return to the school.

Jim and a friend had discussed the possibility of not coming back to the "Blinky" during the last part of their eighth-grade year. Both had decided by the end of school, that this was to be their last year. Though Jim had made up his mind, he let most of the summer pass before announcing his decision to our parents. If they ever had any reservations about the change, they never let them be known to Jim or me.

Mom and Dad wrote a letter to Austin to inform the School for the Bind that Jim would not be returning that year and was planning to attend public school. The head of the school wrote back saying we were making a terrible mistake. Other parents had tried this and had subsequently returned their children to the school after the students found that public school was not geared to meet their needs. A reply of this sort was to be expected, however, and it didn't change the plans in the least.

Overton High School Gets a New Student

In September of 1958, Overton High School enrolled its first totally blind student. Jim's friend, however, had changed his mind and returned to the Blinky. A few days before school was to start that year, Mom took Jim to the school so that he could learn where all the buildings and his classrooms were. The high school campus consisted two separate buildings separated by a long set of concrete steps, a road and more steps down and then up. It was hard enough for a sighted student to negotiate in the rush to get from one class to the next, let alone a blind person. Mom got his schedule, which he copied to Braille, and walked with him to the rooms where he would be going in the order he would be going. They walked the path only two or three times. By the time they returned home that day, Jim knew where all of his classes would be and how to get from one to the next. He now had a map in his mind of most of the important features of the campus. This fact alone was to amaze many of the students who did not know Jim or that he would be on their campus that year. Many were amazed that first day to see this blind stranger making his way from class to class un-assisted.

Jim was aware that he did not know a lot of the kids that would be in his classes. Though he was "known of" by many of the kids, his out of town schooling had not afforded Jim the opportunity to make as many friends in Overton as he would like to have. But Jim knew the importance of friends and was determined that he would take the opportunity to make as many new friends as possible as quickly as he could. Since in those days, teachers had students read aloud in class quite often, Jim had the opportunity to learn the voices of his classmates very quickly. With his acute hearing and voice memory, he could recognize who was talking from very far away. Jim was able to learn the names of his classmates quickly and was able to recognize them and call them by name, forcing from them a response and a chance to communicate with them. It made it harder for his classmates to stand aloof and stare at or comment about the new boy.

One of Jim's worries about changing school was that he might have trouble getting accustomed to his new friends, but he soon realized that exactly the opposite was to be the real problem. Because most of the kids had never been around a blind person other than as a passing acquaintance, they had the problem of getting comfortable around Jim. Most of us do not know how to relate to a person with a handicap, be it blindness, muscular dystrophy, polio or whatever. We tend to try to euphemize the situation, being overly cautious of what we say so as to not accidentally offend. This often calls more attention to the handicap than is necessary. There is no telling how many times someone would stumble for words because they were trying to not offend, such as when they might ask, "Did you wat ... listen to television last night?" Of course, Jim watched television, he watched movies, too, but he only listened to radio. I think it amused him to hear people stumble for words when he did not take offense at the innocent slips that seemed to paralyze the "slippee." He also noticed that some people felt somehow guilty if they said something as innocent as "I'll be seeing you."

The teachers were very accommodating, though none of them had any experience working with blind students. Jim put them at ease with his self-assured attitude and confidence. He asked nothing special of any of his teachers and expected no special favors.

In one class, one of his teachers was using a map to explain where a certain event had occurred. Remembering that Jim was blind, she apologized, "Oh, I'm sorry, Jimmy. You can't see this, can you?"

Jim retorted, "No, ma'am, not from where I'm sitting."

Jim was not trying to be cute or curt, rather he was just trying to put the teacher and classmates at ease, letting them know that he was not sensitive about his blindness.

He quickly realized that taking notes in class in Braille was annoying and distracting to the other students since it required punching dots in thick paper using a stylus and metal tray which made audible clicks. His solution was to record the lessons on tape, replay them at night and make his notes from the tapes or to borrow notes from a friend and transcribe them at home later with the help of Mom or a friend. He had a math tutor who could spend the one-on-one time necessary to explain the problems without interfering with the time the teacher needed in his classroom. Jim had a great mind for math and could work problems in his head that most people couldn't keep up with on paper. Other than that, Jim was just another student. Within a couple of weeks, he had the layout of the school memorized and could walk quite briskly from class to class and building to building with no aides or guides. Within only a few weeks, Jim was no longer the oddity on campus, just another student trying (sometimes not too diligently) to stay out of trouble.

Blind, But NOT Defenseless

Of course, being the only blind kid in town, Jim was an oddity to some, and as in any group, there were those who saw anyone outside the ordinary as an opportunity to taunt and pester. One such person in particular, one known for his toughness and ability on the football field, decided that he could have fun by sneaking up and tapping on Jim's shoulder and quickly darting away from the blind boy, just to see how much of a nuisance he could be. Being new to the world of the blind, especially this blind boy, the lad had failed to learn enough about his victim. First of all, Jim had been on the wrestling team for four years at the School for the Blind and was quite accomplished. Second, thanks to "American Combat Judo", which Jim and I had learned from a book, Jim was more than prepared to handle himself against almost anyone his age. Third the lad was not aware that Jim could hear and identify his approach, even when he, who often wore moccasins, was as sneaky as possible. Finally, Jim had a very short fuse and an explosive temper, especially with people who were testing him because of his blindness.

The day finally came when Jim had given all the requests and warnings he was going to give. When the lad came to pick at the blind boy, Jim wheeled, caught him by the arm and threw him to the ground, parked himself on the lad's chest, pinned his arms to the ground, and had him in position to beat him senseless. After a rather angry lecture on how he was not going to tolerate any more of this type of behavior and that next time would mean a trip to the hospital, Jim let the lad up. He arose from the ground a changed man with a new respect for the blind. With time the lad became one of Jim's friends. From that day on, there were no more "pick on the blind boy stunts" in that school.

The Tennis Tournament

One story that Jim loved to tell about his early years in public school occurred when the district tennis tournament was held at our campus. Players from several schools in the area were gathered at our two courts and as Jim and some of his friends were walking past, a young lady from a neighboring school whispered audibly to her friend, "That boy is blind!"

Jim could hear that whisper from some twenty-five feet away. He stopped, turned his head toward the girls and said loudly, "Yeah! But he isn't deaf." Having mortified them completely, he turned and continued on to class.

While this incident was brief, it was very helpful in understanding what made Jim tick. He never wanted to be recognized as a blind person, only as a person. He took great delight in occasions like this where he could make people stop and think about their own perceptions of others; he in particular and the handicapped in general. If he bumped into someone in the hall on his way to class, he would, as often as not, say, "What's the matter with you, blind or something?" If he tripped and fell he would say something like "I didn't see that hole," spring back to his feet and continue on his way. No one was ever allowed to have the opportunity to show sympathy or feel pity for his inconvenience, and no one was ever allowed to have the satisfaction of having helped this blind boy unless asked to do so.

FRITZ AND THE BLINK: AN OVERTURE TO LIFE

Somebody Speak Up

One evening Jim went over to our uncle's house with the cousins and some friends who were playing pool in the den. One of the friends was not a very good pool player, and after he missed an incredibly easy shot, my uncle said, "You shoot pool like a blind wash woman." The entire room went dead silent, fearing that Jim was going to take offense to the remark. After allowing sufficient time for guilt to build in all in the room, Jim pronounced loudly, "It sure got quiet in here." The ice broke; everyone laughed. Jim, of course, was not offended, but people are funny that way; they feel guilty when they fear they just stuck their foot in their mouth.

Fore!

Jim played miniature golf at the course that Dad and a friend owned in the park, and Jim was a fairly good putter. A companion would tap the metal cup with his club head, and Jim would line up on the sound for direction and distance and putt. He was actually pretty good, but had a short temper, as all golfers do. If he were having a bad game, a true golfer's attitude would cause him to pound his putter to the ground and utter certain phrases commonly heard on golf courses. He also liked to go to the driving range and drive balls. He was strong as an ox and would knock the cover off the ball but he had trouble "keeping his eye on the ball" and often hooked and sliced miserably.

At the insistence of a friend, Jim one day went to the municipal golf course with him to play "real" golf. *"On one occasion, I had gotten pretty far down the fairway and was waiting for him to catch up. When he finally did, I told him that he might as well go ahead, so he could go on down the course and let me know which way to shoot, which he did. After hitting his ball for some distance, he headed on up the fairway and told me to just hit toward his voice. After giving warning, to deaf ears, incidentally, that I could hit farther than he* expected, I gave the ball a whack that sent it into a hard, wild hook. There followed shortly a loud thud and a grunt that was of both pain and surprise. It didn't take long to figure out that I had hit him in the back."

It must have been quite a sight. Jim later confessed that neither of them had any more business on a golf course than a ditch digger. Jim realized that and stopped playing golf, but his friend continued to terrorize the links for several years. Jim never did establish his handicap on the golf course, but he did replay the Goliath and David story with a new weapon and victim.

Cracking More than Jokes

In his senior year, Jim's class was joined by a new boy who had not had the opportunity to grow up around Jim. He was a rather annoying personality to Jim because he liked to give the punch lines when another person was telling a joke. This did not set well with Jim, who loved to tell jokes, possessed a great sense of timing and could embellish a story to get the maximum humor from it. On several occasions, the lad had been warned by Jim to stop his habit. However, some people are slow learners. The Day of Judgment finally came. On this occasion, Jim had been with a small group of friends in the hall of the school between classes telling jokes. The boy had given the punch line away two times and had received his final warning. As the third joke neared completion, he ignored the warnings and started to give the punch line. He was stopped in mid-sentence as a fist came from Jim's waist directly to his forehead ending the interruption abruptly. There was no further altercation, only the sound of a hard head bouncing off the hall floor. The ambulance had to be called to carry the victim of a concussion to the hospital for observation. Jim never had his punch line stolen again after he re-defined "punch" line.

FRITZ AND THE BLINK: AN OVERTURE TO LIFE

Eating Well Was a Cohagen Tradition

Eating was another activity that approached an art form in my family. My mother grew up during the depression when meat on the table was a special occasion. She did, however, have a learned knack for cooking vegetables. My father's dad was a farmer, so Mom and Dad didn't starve, and Mom was a great cook. She could make vegetables alone seem like the finest dinner anyone could ever want. Dad on the other hand was a meat and potatoes man. He always claimed that he was twelve years old before he found out that gravy was not a part of a chicken. He also was a very good cook, specializing in meats: roasted, fried, grilled, broiled or barbecued.

On one trip to Austin to pick up Jim from school, we happened upon an overturned eighteen-wheeler. It was carrying dairy products, and several tons of real butter were scattered across and around the highway. Dad quickly drove to the nearest town and bought a double-ought washtub and some ice. We returned to the scene quickly and with the blessing of the highway patrol did our part to help clean the debris off the highway. We brought home about two hundred pounds of real butter. Dad bought a butter press and packed the bulk butter into one pound blocks and took them to the local locker plant where they were frozen until needed. Margarine had just made its debut, but our family ate nothing but real butter for the next four or five years.

Dad did have a way with barbecue. An old black man had given him a "secret" recipe for his special sauce and had him swear to keep it a secret, which he did for many years before passing it on to me. One of the special ingredients was real butter, which we had no shortage of. I am proud to say that I now have that recipe and still consider it the best cooking sauce I have ever used. It may have been that sauce that created my appreciation for fine barbecue; an appreciation shared by my brother. We considered ourselves connoisseurs of fine barbecue and learned quickly that white men could not touch the flavor of the black man's specialty.

JOHN R. COHAGEN

Shack Was a Man as Well as a Place

Our favorite place to get barbecue was from a colored gentleman known as "Shack." "Shack" was very old, nearly blind, and worn with years, but he had a knack for barbecue that made him a legend among the barbecue crowd. His restaurant was a small lean-to of salvaged lumber and rusty corrugated tin located far off the main road near his home. The "shack" from which he had gained his nickname, was barely eight feet square and maybe six feet high. Inside he had an old barbecue pit made from a fifty-five gallon drum, a small table on which he prepared his sandwiches and a chair where he sat waiting for customers to come by. A roll of paper towels provided napkins, towels, and wrappers for the sandwiches he made. A wash tub with ice cooled the drinks he kept for his customers. The greatest thing of all was the aroma of the hickory fire and the cooking meat that filled the air for miles downwind from that shack.

Now "Shack" was an agreeable old gentleman, though nearly deaf as well as almost blind. Placing an order was a time-honored ordeal of very loud talking, filling "Shack" with the latest gossip, and watching as he deftly scraped the hot, dripping fat off the brisket he had just pulled off the pit and cut up the lean meat for the sandwich. I think that cutting is the wrong word, because you could slice his tender meat with the backside of a butter knife. At any rate, he would chop or slice the brisket into a large mound of meat then pile it high on white bread, and cover it with his special sauce.

Shack had a special fondness for Jim, and always made his sandwich a little thicker than everyone else's. If I ever went there without Jim, he would want to know where he was and how he was doing.

Our love for barbecue however was not limited to the marvelous feasts we enjoyed at the shack. Anytime we were out at night and in unfamiliar territory, we would search out a new barbecue stand, preferably one owned by a black man since we knew the chances of getting better barbecue were greater at these places. I must take a second to point out that this was occurring in the early '60s, a time when it was considered extremely improper to associate with people of the "other race." Jim and I, however, lacked both prejudice and good sense when it came to barbecue.

Jim never concerned himself that there was a difference in people because of their skin color. Everybody was the same color to him. The racial situation in the South was very tense in the early '60s, and it could have had created serious problems for two white boys who might put themselves in a situation that wasn't particularly safe just to get a barbecue sandwich. Because we lacked prejudice, we believed that was, or at least should have been, the prevailing attitude of everyone. However, that was not the case in rural East Texas and our innocence could have caused serious problems had the Lord not kept such a good eye out for us.

Midnight Is a Bad Time to Want Barbecue

On one memorable evening, Jim and I were returning from a football game on a road that we rarely traveled. Jim's nose smelled the aroma of barbecue coming from an old building we had just passed, and he began demanding that we turn back immediately and get a sandwich. I was hungry, too, and turned around. It was well after eleven p.m. and no one was outside the building, but cars were parked all around and the smell of some fine barbecue lingered in the night air. The barbecue smelled so good that it overrode any thoughts we had of how stupid we were to be going into a strange place in the middle of the night. When we opened the door and started in, it was like a scene from *Animal House*. Jim and I were the only two white people in the place; it was a very exclusive atmosphere. As Jim would say, "We felt like cobras at a Mongoose Convention." All activity suddenly ceased and every eye in the place turned to look at us. There was only one smile to be seen, and the smile belonged to a man holding a butcher knife.

In absolute silence we walked up to the counter and ordered two sandwiches, TO GO. The man with the butcher knife carved out the meat, placed it on the buns, added his special sauce, wrapped the sandwiches, bagged them and set them on the counter. We paid for our sandwiches and made our way back through the silent dining area and out the door. The sandwiches were excellent, though I ate mine while driving. I swore a silent oath that I would not be stopping there again.

The Night Lightning Struck

One other occasion where barbecue played a key part in our adventures occurred later that same year. Jim was dating a young lady from Longview, and I had gone to pick him up from her house and bring him home. As always, Jim was hungry, but we knew Shack would not be open because it was already nearly midnight. On the way home we passed a black barbecue stand in Kilgore. It was still open and many people were standing around the serving window enjoying barbecue. We had never eaten there before, but decided to give it a shot. The name of the place was Lightnin's. It was a larger building than Shack's, but made of much of the same materials, so we felt comfortable with the atmosphere.

We walked up to the window and ordered our sandwiches. "Lightnin" was a very friendly fellow and visited with us as he cut up the meat and stacked it high on the buns. "What kind of barbecue sauce do you want; mild, medium, or hot?" This was a new experience for us, normally at a barbecue stand, the pride of the cook was his special sauce; you took that or none. We had never had to make a choice like this before.

"Hot," Jim declared confidently.

"OK," said "Lightnin" with a strange smile on his face. He poured on the sauce, topped the heaping sandwiches with the other halves of the buns, wrapped them in tissue paper, and handed them out the window. As we paid for the sandwiches and Big Orange drinks, he added with a chuckle, "Most white boys don't like my hot sauce."

"I like it hot!" Jim declared.

That night, "hot" took on a whole new meaning. About half way through my sandwich, my Big Orange had been exhausted. It took two more to finish the sandwich and cool my mouth and throat down. Jim fared little better, but his stubbornness would allow him to have only one more Big Orange, rather than to have to admit in front of strangers that he thought the sauce was too hot. We burned all the way home, laughing and joking about how "we like it hot" while still wiping the sweat from our faces.

We did eat at Lightnin's again, several times, but our next orders included his mild sauce.

Flattery Makes Friends

Glenda was in Jim's class in high school, and she was one of Jim's special friends. She had a marvelous sense of humor and enjoyed Jim's stories and gags. She related to me an incident that happened in the hall between classes. Jim was walking down the hall and passed Glenda's locker where she was gathering her books for the next class. She did not speak, nor was she walking, but as Jim got near, he turned his head toward her and said, "How are you today, Glenda?"

She was startled. "How did you know I was here?" she asked.

"Because you smell SO good," Jim replied. With that Jim created a memory and strengthened a friendship.

I Love Winning Arguments

Jim's quick mind and competitive nature made him a perfect debater. He and his partners made several trips the Regional Contest and one trip to the State Meet. Jim was not above using every advantage to win his arguments. A special ploy of his was to take notes of his opponents' speeches in Braille using a metal guide and stylus to punch the dots in the special thick paper. The resulting noise of the click and pop of the stylus as it punched the paper was a major distraction to his opponent as he tried to present his case. In truth, Jim was not taking notes; he kept them in his head. He was only writing nonsense to create the distraction. After all, who would know; he was the only one in the room who could read Braille.

I Love Winning Bets, Too!

During his senior year, Jim was boasting that he could walk home by himself if he wanted to. A few of his friends decided that they would have to see that to believe it. The boast became more of a bet and several of the students put up money to force Jim's hand. Jim had never walked home by himself before, but on numerous occasions he and I had walked home after school, so he was quite familiar with the route. Most of his friends were aware of how well he could navigate the crowded hallways of the school, but just could not know that Jim's head was filled with maps of the entire city, developed over the years he and I had walked the streets together.

Jim happily covered any bet his friends wanted to lose and at the end of school that day, he and a group of doubting Thomases gathered at the front of the school to see if Jim could truly find his way home. Our house was about a mile away from the school, and Jim struck out, full of confidence with a gaggle of geese following a short distance behind.

In less than twenty minutes, Jim was at home, collecting his money from the suckers who thought he couldn't do it. The losers were not sore, just awed, because on the way home, Jim had successfully made all the necessary turns, and also avoided collisions with parked cars, which he could hear as they echoed his footsteps. The feat was probably made easier because of the crowd that was following him. They probably were commenting on things that gave him clues that they didn't realize were helping him get where he was going. One thing I am sure of, he played it to the hilt, for Jim was a showman and knew how to make the most of any situation.

FRITZ AND THE BLINK: AN OVERTURE TO LIFE

Recognition

Some of Jim's fondest stories of high school life were not about himself, but about his friends. One such story involved a friend and a visiting science demonstrator. The demonstrator was presenting his show in chemistry class. He reached into a box and brought out a strange-looking glass object and asked, "Have any of you ever seen a cathode ray tube?"

The class was silent, kids looking at each other, then the friend spoke out, "Is that one in your hand?"

"Why, yes, it is," declared the demonstrator.

The friend immediately raised his hand, waving it around to indicate that he had seen one.

Unofficial Cheerleader

Like any other red blooded Texan, Jim loved football. No, he didn't play, but he loved to go to the high school games where his friends were playing. He loved the electric atmosphere, the noise, the bands, and the sound of human bodies colliding with great force. He could ascertain very accurately what was going on out on the playing field, and at the same time entertained those around him with his loud yells and impromptu cheers, the likes of which no self respecting cheerleader would dare utter. One of his favorite cheers went something like this:

Rickety Rackity Russ
We're not allowed to cuss
But never the less
We must confess,
Can't no damned team beat us.

The principal did not approve of that particular yell, so Jim changed the last line to fit the more conservative standards of the day while exuding the culture and refinement of a college-bound student. That last line became:

We shall not succumb to any team of the condemned nature.
Another favorite cheer:
Chew tobacco, Chew tobacco,
Spit, Spit, Spit
Exlax, Exlax,
Go! Go! Go!

That cheer raised a few eyebrows, especially at away games where people were experiencing Jim for the first time.

Supporting the Team

The football team in 1962, Jim's senior year, was awesome. In the regular season that year the team scored over 500 points to their opponents 50 or so. Jim's enthusiasm for the game sparked his imagination. He wanted to do something to provide an outlet for his enthusiasm and show his support for the team. Our biggest rivalry was with Leverett's Chapel, a school only three miles away from Overton, and Jim devised a plan to give a boost to the team.

About two nights before the big game, Jim and I, along with our girlfriends at the time, loaded up several gallons of gasoline and drove to Leverett's Chapel football stadium. Our original intent was to burn a big "O" in the center of the field on the fifty-yard line. When we arrived late that night, all was quiet, so we carried the gas cans to the center of the field. Jim stood on the exact center of the field, an anchor in the center of what was to become the big "O." We all held hands, Jim, the two girls and me on the outside with the gas cans. We slowly walked in a circle around Jim as I poured gasoline on the grass. When all the gasoline was gone, we made probably our best decision; that was to not light the gasoline, but rather just let it kill the grass over the next few days. A fire would have probably been seen and we would have been caught. So we loaded up our cans and left.

That Friday night when we went to the game to root the team on to victory, we were pleased to see a yellow-brown "O" of dead and dying grass in the center of the field. While it sparked our team, it also made for an interesting game. The opposing team did not share our appreciation for the symbol we had wrought.

FRITZ AND THE BLINK: AN OVERTURE TO LIFE

The Victory Bell

Later that year, as it became apparent that the team was going to the playoffs, Jim and his friends decided that more inspiration was needed. They thought it would be a great idea for the team to have a victory bell, which could be rung after the team scored a touchdown or field goal. This surely would liven up the game and bring recognition to the team. Finding an appropriate bell at a price they could afford took some doing, but they finally came up with what they thought was the perfect bell. There was only one minor hitch. The bell was already claimed by the congregation of a small Negro church some distance from town. Not willing to let a small thing like this stand in their way, about five of them decided that by the time the sun rose on a new morning, that bell would be our team's official victory bell. They all piled in a car and headed for the spot, expecting to bring back the sought prize.

Little brothers were not invited for this raid, but the story was retold so vividly and so often, that I feel like I was there. When they arrived at the bell, they became somewhat apprehensive, for the bell was quite a bit larger than they had thought. It would take some doing to get it down from its place on top of a pole, which stood seven feet tall. The boys regrouped and came up with quite a clever plan of attack. The bell was mounted on the pole in such a way that all a person had to do to get it was to push up under it until he had raised it off the mountings, and then the bell would fall to the ground. The plan was well thought out. They all made a wild dash for the pole and mounted their assault. However, nature was about to give them a big surprise.

The first to reach the bell and the first to try to lay a hand on it got a little more than he bargained for. At the same moment his hand came in contact with the bell, there was a bright flash of light in the heavens. "Someone had spotted us and turned on the spotlights," was the thought that flashed through their heads. For just a minute everyone was still and then everybody broke into a dead run for the car—everybody, that is, except for Jim. He didn't have the slightest idea of what had happened, but it didn't take long for him to get the message that something was amiss and, following the sounds of the frantic footsteps of his friends, he headed in the general direction of the car, too.

By this time, lights had begun to come on in the community, for they weren't the only ones who had been taken by surprise by the strange flash of light.

After some careful consideration, they decided that the thing must have been a meteor. If they were going to get the bell, they would have to wait until the people of the community reached the same conclusion and went back to bed. Since they had not been spotted, they hid out in their car until things calmed down.

In a short time the calm was restored, and the boys decided it was safe to return to the task at hand. This time, however, they were a bit more cautious. They decided to inspect the bell just a bit more closely. The inspection revealed a bunch of wasps that had nested inside the bell, which would make it almost impossible to get the bell without getting stung. They finally decided to give up the idea of bringing home the bell that night and but settled on an alternate prank.

What fun it would be to give the local folks, a real scare. They decided that the ringing of the bell, especially after the mysterious bright flash of light in the night, might just do the trick. The wasps made the usual means of ringing the bell out of the question since someone would more than likely be stung. They soon struck upon a plan which would do nicely. Each of them gathered as many of the large rocks as they could hold. These were readily available from the iron ore parking lot. On a given signal they began heaving them at the bell. At the same time all began yelling, "Dee Lord's coming! Dee Lord's coming!"

Lights, which had been turned out some time before, were now suddenly reappearing. Dogs, which had not been disturbed by the flash, awoke and began barking at the disturbance. A few of the braver souls finally opened their doors just enough to get a good look outside to see what the trouble was. A hasty retreat was made to the car and away from the community.

FRITZ AND THE BLINK: AN OVERTURE TO LIFE

A few minutes later they drove back through the community and had to laugh at the people of the community who were still out investigating the situation, trying to figure out just what had caused that strange disturbance in the night.

Target: The Band Director

Jim loved the football team and Jim loved the band, but he could not claim the same respect for the band director, who was not liked by many of the students. One day Jim and a few of his friends were standing on the hill behind the gym, shooting the bull, as the band was practicing on the football field below. They were discussing how much they did not like the band director, a discussion that was being lead and carried by Jim. The more they talked, the more upset Jim became. Finally, Jim decided it was time to act. One of the boys had a football, which Jim demanded be given to him. He was going to throw it from the hill and hit the band director who was some seventy-five yards away on the field. No one thought Jim would actually do this, so they let him have the ball.

Each time the band director blew his whistle or shout directions, Jim would listen carefully, focusing his radar ears to ascertain the direction and distance necessary for his mighty toss. TWEET! Adjust. TWEET! Adjust. Each successive whistle brought the target into clearer focus. Unknown to Jim, just as he was preparing to wind up and heave his greatest pass, the principal, the superintendent, and a coach walked around the corner of the gym and saw Jim cocking his arm to throw. Immediately, they perceived the intended target, and as they didn't like the band director any more than most of the students, they took the only course of action open to them. Turning on their heels, almost like a military formation, all three turned their backs to the situation and walked briskly back around the corner of the gym just as Jim let the football fly.

No! He did not hit his target, but his aim was only off by about ten feet, close enough to make his point but far enough to avoid serious consequences.

Don't Touch the Hat!

Jim did love to go to the football games. He often dressed in unique clothes to draw attention to himself. Somewhere, Jim had acquired a hat that he loved to wear to football games, just because it was controversial. It was pointed, woven-straw hat, similar in appearance to the hat worn by Chico Marx, except it had a long turkey feather in the back and Confederate flags on each side. On the front it said, "Forget? Hell, No!" Jim was not a racist; the hat did not carry that connotation for him. Rather it expressed his spirit as a rebel, not so much against the North, but against society in general and its attitude toward handicapped persons. The hat certainly stood out in a crowd and drew attention to him. That, I think, was its primary purpose. Whatever the purpose, you didn't fool with his hat.

I made the mistake of doing that one night at a ball game. I was standing behind him and tipped the hat on his head. He turned around and hit me in the stomach, sending me two rows up the bleachers. I felt the action was quite severe, but it made his case, and I was careful to avoid touching his hat again.

A Real Ham

Because Mom was the speech, English and drama teacher at our high school, both of us were active in plays and were never afraid to appear on stage. Jim could memorize lines about as fast as anyone I have ever known, and once he had a map of the stage in his head, he could get around as easily as anyone else could. He was never in a contest play, but did appear in many skits, one-acts, and musicals. He was also an accomplished public speaker and spoke at banquets and church gatherings and entertained with his singing and jokes.

A Ham Off the Stage, Too

Jim became interested in ham radio while at the School for the Blind, where a friend he had met would take him out occasionally to play Fox and Hound. A mobile radio operator would be given a lead time in which to go hide. Beginning at a specified time, he would have to transmit for a certain length of time at regular intervals. Other operators would try to locate his position by using directional antennas and maps to triangulate his location. The first to find the Fox was the winner. Jim loved this game, but had no one to play it with after he moved back home.

An army buddy of Dad's gave him a complete short-wave receiver and Jim acquired a transmitter shortly afterwards. His room became his ham-radio station. When he was not studying, or playing his guitar, Jim spent many late night hours talking all around the world to others through Morse code and later by voice. In this way he made friends all over the United States and abroad who never saw him and probably never knew he was blind, as it would not have been part of his conversations.

The Blind Leading the Blind Leading the Blind

Jim's friend, Benis, also liked electronics. When Jim decided he wanted to build an amplifier from a kit, he enticed Benis to help him. The kit was bought and the two boys started to build. Jim understood electronics, Benis could read schematics and do the assembly, but one little problem had been overlooked. Jim was totally blind and Benis was color-blind. Electronic components are color-coded. Neither of them could tell what resister or capacitor to use. Guess who got called into the project next? Little brother came to the rescue. I knew nothing about electronics. All I could do was look at the color bands on the parts and try to match the color sequences on them to the sequences given on the schematic diagrams as Benis would read the printed color codes from the diagram. The Three Musketeers made a valiant attempt at the assembly, but the amplifier never got completed and eventually was scrapped.

JOHN R. COHAGEN

His Choice Had Been a Good One

All in all, Jim's high school experience was great for him. He was in the speech club, on the debate team, president of the Spanish Club, in the Honor Society, president of the student council, and valedictorian. He loved learning, studying, reading, but most of all, he loved life and his high school buddies saw to it that he had ample opportunity to do so, creating memories not only for Jim, but for them, too. His close friends never thought of him as handicapped. His friends just recognized that he was blessed with a love of life that was outrageous and contagious. They just enjoyed the opportunity to share that love of life with him.

Filled with high hopes and dreams, Jim made plans to go to Kilgore Jr. College the following fall, having finished his life's Overture and ready for Act I.

FRITZ AND THE BLINK: AN OVERTURE TO LIFE

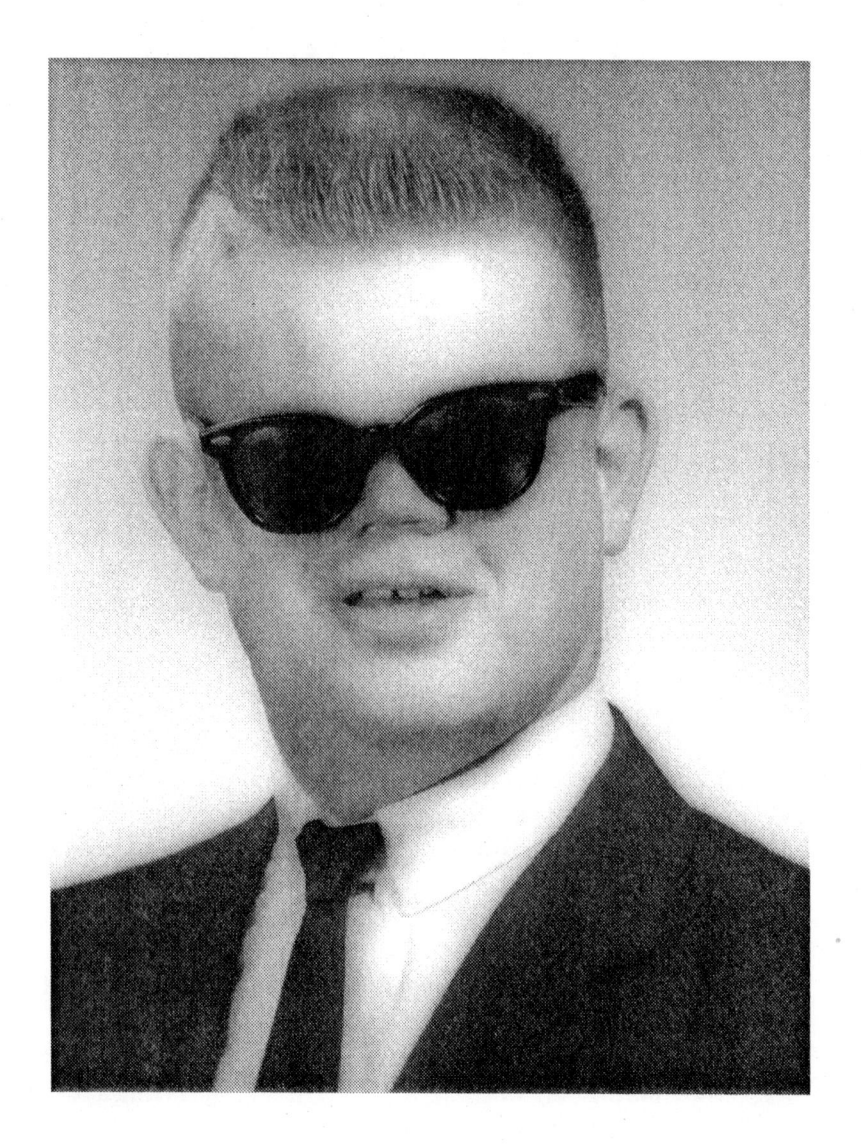

Senior Portrait

— Chapter 9 —
Testing the Limits

In many ways, Jim was like Chuck Yeager, Scott Crossfield and other great test pilots. He pushed his life experiences the same way they would push an airplane to find the limits of its flight envelope. He wanted to be able to exact every measure of life that was possible for him and would often push new situations to failure just to know how far he could go.

Jim and I had two very distinct personalities. He was hard as a rock, stubborn and very confident. I, on the other hand, was tender, submissive and easily intimidated. This was very apparent when we were children. Our parents were strict disciplinarians when the need arose though they were very permissive in allowing us to explore and develop our own personalities. The best description of us as children was given by one of our babysitters. She was trying to use tact to describe her experience with us as she told Mom and Dad, "Your children are certainly…er…uh…um…uninhibited." I didn't know exactly what she meant by that at the time, though I was reminded of it time and again as Mom loved to tell that story to her friends. The best I could make out, it meant something between mischievous and totally out of control.

While I might agree with mischievous, Jim and I were rarely out of control. Like the time when we were very young and taking a bath together. We discovered that if we rocked back and forth in unison, the water would also begin to follow our movements and create a large tidal wave that would move from end to end. We thought that this was a very clever discovery and spent several minutes creating a mini tsunami in the tub. The fact that the water was splashing over the sides as it hit the end of the tub, however, did escape our attention since we were fully concentrating on the wave action.

That fact did not go unnoticed by our parents as the water began to flow under the bathroom door and out into the hall. We were suddenly and rudely apprised of the mistake we were making. While still in our birthday suits, we were hoisted to a standing position on the lid of the commode and spanked with a belt. The difference in our reactions to that spanking illustrates the differences in our personalities.

Even before the first swat was applied to my dripping bottom, I was crying and screaming for mercy, large tears pouring from my eyes. Jim on the other hand, just gritted his teeth, took his beating in absolute silence and never shed a tear. Later when we were in bed, Jim rebuked me for being such a crybaby. This was basically his attitude toward any punishment that he would ever receive in the future. If he knew he had messed up and been caught, he simply bowed up his neck, accepted the consequences and went on his way. He did learn from the experience, but he would never give anyone the satisfaction of believing that they could hurt him. This was a mental toughness that I admired, but would not develop for many years to come.

I think that part of Jim's attitude was based around his idea that he knew he would have to test the limits with other people all of his life, and that sometimes in testing the limits he might go a little too far before he discovered where that limit was. Punishment was to him just a part of that process, but would not be a deterrent to pushing the envelope to the limits. This attitude helped Jim to become the person that people admired. NO FEAR was a phrase that had not yet been coined, but it was the attitude Jim exhibited when exploring a new situation.

The Early Test

A college friend of Jim's shared a story with me that I had never heard before. Jim had shared the story with him in confidence. It seems that while at the school for the blind, Jim and a friend had attempted shoplifting at a store just off the campus. Whatever they took they would return on another trip, but they did it just to see if a blind person could do it. Jim did not have a criminal nature rather this was just one of his attempt to test the limits of his limitations as a blind person. Future tests were more honest and more interesting, often outlandish and daring, sometimes bordering on stupid. These challenges to the norm, in my opinion, were absolutely necessary for Jim. He used each new trial as a confirmation of his ability to overcome the perception of being handicapped that other people often felt until they got to know him better.

Growing up with Jim, I never thought about many of the things we did together as pushing the limits. We just did things that amazed other people who did not know us well, but we just took it for granted that we were supposed to be able to do them. When our attempts at new limits failed, we often ended up with a few bruises or scrapes, but I never recall a time when Jim and I were reprimanded for trying something new or slightly dangerous. We were often warned of certain dangers and reminded sometimes of our previous failures, but I think they knew the necessity of Jim exploring his limits, and as nerve-racking as it must have been, they allowed us the freedom to do that. I am sure that my parents and their friends could recall many stories that would fit into this category, things we did as youngsters, which to us at the time didn't seem so extraordinary. Unfortunately that generation is gone now and those stories are lost forever.

I did have a lady tell me recently that she remembered seeing Jim and me running up the street in front of her house when we were kids, and was amazed how Jim was able to run like that when he was blind. To me, this was no amazing feat. We often walked and ran all over this area. Running was one of our favorite methods of transportation. Jim would start beside me with his left hand lightly touching my right arm. Once we reached our pace, he would let go and run beside me using the sounds of my footsteps and conversation to maintain his relative position. We grew up doing this and never thought of it as anything difficult or amazing. About the only problem we had was avoiding the many potholes that were in our small town streets. An occasional skinned knee and palm from falling on the rough street were just part of the routine.

One habit we had did cause our parents a little concern. When walking on a main street, we chose the center stripe as our path. Our logic was that if we walked in the middle, we would be more visible to drivers from both directions and therefore less likely to be hit by mistake. Mom and Dad unfortunately did not agree with our logic and made us break the habit.

The most outlandish tests of limits occurred in our high school years and these stories I remember well because some of them even amazed me.

Up Periscope

When Jim was in High school, Dad had a 1948 Ford Pickup. It wasn't a great ride, but it was available for Jim's friends to use when they wanted to take Jim somewhere. On one occasion, Jim and his buddy, Mitch, were just riding around with nothing much in particular on their minds. Jim began to tell Mitch that he would like to drive the truck. Well, that didn't seem too ridiculous to them at the time. Jim was familiar with the gear pattern of a stick on the floor, having been my co-pilot on several occasions, in charge of changing the gears when I worked the clutch and drove. On occasions, I had let Jim have a hand at the steering wheel, though I remained in the driver's seat and he only turned the wheel, as I would call out directions. "Left, right, a little more." I could always take over when we started to run off the road or met on-coming traffic. This was not what Jim had in mind. He wanted to DRIVE the truck.

I must point out that I was not a participant in what happened that day, though I unknowingly supplied a vital piece of hardware that made it possible. I had a fascination with optics, and had a large collection of mirrors, magnifying glasses, prisms and a tank periscope that I had bought at an Army Surplus store. It had a nice, wide field of vision and crystal clear optics. I used it to peek around corners and over fences in order to surprise my friends. The use that Jim and Mitch had in mind was much more creative.

The East Texas oilfield had left many scars in the area. There were places called salt flats where the salt water used to drill wells was dumped out to evaporate. The salt in the water was left behind and killed all vegetation leaving large, open, flat areas of ground. While I do not know this as a fact, I suspect that it was on one of these salt flats where Mitch taught Jim how to drive the truck, since there were no obstacles to run into.

At this time, Dad was a rural route carrier for the U.S. post office and carried the mail on Route 1, Overton. A friend of Dad's named Gene, who also happened to live across the street from us and who had known Jim all of his life, carried Route 2. It was on the oil-topped back roads of Route 2 where Mitch and Jim decided to try a little road trip.

With Jim behind the wheel and Mitch hunkered down in the floorboard, peering over the dash with my tank periscope, the adventure began. I don't know how far or how fast the trip actually was, but it was long enough to meet Gene making his mail deliveries. Gene saw the truck coming down the road, recognized it, and thinking he was meeting Dad, stuck his hand out the window to give a wave of greeting. His hand turned clammy, his skin white, as he recognized the driver of the truck. He pulled off the road, obviously shaken, and watched as the truck passed by. He continued sitting there for almost half an hour before he felt comfortable enough to continue his route.

That afternoon, when Gene returned to the office, Dad was already there, sorting his mail for the next day. Gene came in, still a little shaken, and said, "Arnold, you aren't going to believe this! I saw Jimmy driving your truck out on my route."

"I believe it," replied Dad in a matter-of-fact tone and returned calmly to his mail sorting. By this time, I guess Dad had lost the ability to be surprised by anything Jim might do with his friends. When Dad got home that day, Jim and Mitch were there in Jim's room, playing their guitars and singing merrily. There was a discussion about what had happened, but more laughing than yelling. I believe the recounting of the look on Gene's face as seen through a periscope made anger impossible.

The Traffic Stopper

Evidently the joy of driving was habit forming, for Jim found other occasions to get behind the wheel. In a small town, kids can get away with just about anything as long as no real harm is done. Unlike in larger towns, the policeman was someone you knew and who knew your family. A small town thrives on the oddities that occur as they provide fodder for the rumor mill. In a small town the news is not necessarily what happened as much as what people say happened and with Jim on the loose there was always something to talk about. Another advantage of a small town is that you only have one policeman on duty at any given time and when he passes by on his rounds, you know that it will be a while before he returns.

Taking advantage of that well-known fact, Jim and his friends would know when it was "safe" to let Jim drive. On several occasions, Jim would take the wheel of Mom's pride and joy, her 1962 convertible Falcon. With the top down, for the entire world to see, he would drive down the main street of Overton waving at the people he met while receiving directions from a friend in the passenger's seat. You can imagine the shock that people who knew Jim must have felt to see such a sight, but no one bothered to report this to the police, though reports did make it home to our parents who somehow accepted that this could and did happen. I guess that is one of my parents' greatest attributes; they understood the fine line between a quest for independence and stupidity that Jim and I often treaded heavily upon.

When friends asked Jim how he could drive a car, Jim would explain, "I just stick my foot out of the door and feel for the curb."

Hot Dogs!

It was a cold, rainy night and the bridge club had our house full of adults. Jim and Mitch wanted to get away from the crowded atmosphere, so they decided they needed to take a trip over to Kilgore and get something to eat. Dad gave Mitch the keys to the old '48 Ford pickup, and they went on their way. Bridge club continued and I was home alone without a date.

About two hours later, the front door burst open. There in the portal stood Jim and Mitch, sopping wet, with feet and legs covered with mud. Mitch had a look of horror on his face, like a cat caught with a canary feather sticking out of his mouth. Jim was right behind him with a huge grin on his face. There was a little commotion but soon the two soggy travelers revealed the reason for their appearance.

On the way home, on a straight section of wet road, they had met a car that was crowding the center line. To avoid the car his friend pulled a little too far to the right shoulder to insure clearance. The right front tire had run off the road into the muddy shoulder. In an effort to get off the shoulder, his friend over-corrected and the truck went into a spin. The truck made three complete revolutions, described in great detail by the still shaking friend and to the sounds of laughter by Jim at the description. The truck then slid backward down a steep embankment into a twelve-foot deep, muddy ditch. They had to climb out of the muddy ditch and walk a pretty good distance before someone came along and gave them a ride to the house.

Dad assured Jim's friend that he wasn't mad, only happy that no one was hurt. He assured him that is why he had insurance. Then Dad called a wrecker to pull the truck out of the ditch. Jim's only concern was that he had left a couple of hot dogs in the seat of the truck, and he wanted to retrieve them before they got cold.

The truck was retrieved, undamaged but muddy. Jim and his nervous friend drove it home where the now cold hot dogs were heated in the oven and eventually met their intended destiny.

FRITZ AND THE BLINK: AN OVERTURE TO LIFE

Cruisin' for a Bruisin'

On one pretty Sunday afternoon, Jim and several of his friends got Mom's Falcon convertible to ride around in with the top down and enjoy the sunshine. They cruised Overton, but nothing was happening. They left town to cruise Kilgore, but nothing was happening there either. They decided to go farther, so they headed to Marshall to see if they could find any excitement. On the way, they happened to drive a little fast and were stopped by a local cop in a small town. He began questioning the boys as to their reason for being where they were in a fashion that seemed to Jim to be a little unnecessarily rude. When the officer asked why they were riding around in his particular area, Jim blurted out, "We just wanted to look at the country." The rest of the boys were mortified and scared at the prospect that the remark would upset the already rude policeman. One of the passengers recalled later that he wanted to strangle Jim to shut him up.

The Incredible Chevy II

Being a rural route carrier, and the father of two teenagers, Dad went through a lot of cars. About two years was all a car would last on the rough and dusty back roads of East Texas under the daily grind of stop and go driving. My driving habits did not exactly extend the life of his vehicles either. Dad tried many cars, looking for the perfect mail car. His current favorite was a 1962 Chevy II Nova, with the larger of the two six-cylinder engines available at that time. The car got great gas mileage, had plenty of pep, and was small enough to be driven from the center of the front seat, as was the custom of mail carriers in those days.

Dad had a friend who was an independently wealthy individual thanks to some family land around Lubbock, which was much better at producing oil than cotton. He was not one of those people who let the fact that he had money make him a snob. He was very down to earth and very friendly, but not having to work for a living, he had plenty of time to keep up with everything that was going on in town. He did, however, have an opinion about everything and was more than willing to share it with anyone, whether they wanted to know or not. Oldsmobile 88's were his car of choice and he could not understand why anyone would drive anything else. Dad decided it was time to introduce his friend to the virtues of the Chevy II.

One day Dad had to make a quick trip to Dallas and invited his friend to ride along to keep him company. Before leaving town Dad stopped at the small store near our house to fill up the car for the trip. The gas pump was located on a pretty good incline, so Dad pulled up the tank in such a way that the gas fill spout was up the hill to allow him to put in the maximum amount of gas that the tank could hold.

All the way to Dallas and back, his friend talked about cars. Numerous questions concerning the Chevy II and many comments about how the Olds 88 was far superior were made. His friend's talking ceased when they got home and Dad went back to the same store to re-fill his tank and calculate his gas mileage. This time, however, Dad approached the pump from the opposite direction so that the gas filler spout was on the low side of the car and the tank when filled would contain a large entrapped air bubble, causing it to appear being filled several gallons short of its maximum capacity. This detail went unnoticed by his friend who was only interested in the mileage figures. In this position, the tank would only take about two and a half gallons. The trip to Dallas and back was about two hundred and fifty miles. When the calculations were made, they showed the mileage for that trip was close to one hundred miles to the gallon. Dad's only comment was, "I bet your Oldsmobile doesn't get mileage like that." No other explanation was ever given, though his friend did comment often about Dad's good mileage.

The little Chevy II actually got around twenty-five miles per gallon and Dad was very proud of that. Suddenly one day, his mileage dropped to around seventeen miles per gallon. He took it back to the dealer and to several mechanics to find out why this had happened. None of them could come up with an explanation for the sudden drop in efficiency. A few months later, the little car was in a wreck, which is described later, and Dad traded for a Ford Falcon and began getting good mileage on the mail route again. It wasn't until about twenty years later that I learned the truth about the mysterious loss of mileage.

A couple of years later Dad retold the story of Hiram and the Chevy II and wistfully mentioned the sudden loss of mileage. It was then that I shared with him the real reason. Jim's friend Daren often used the Chevy II when he and Jim would have their nights out. Being a better than average shade-tree mechanic and a lover of drag racing, Daren was quick to realize that because of the little car's light weight and large engine, it was a perfect car for the drag strip. He and Jim regularly took the car to the strip and had won several trophies with it. They had even gone so far as to buy an extra set of wheels with racing slicks, which they would take to the strip and use for racing to keep from burning up Dad's tires. As good as the little car was, Daren wanted to make it better. He removed the carburetor and drilled out the fuel ports to allow more gas to get to the engine, effectively increasing the horsepower, but reducing the average gas mileage by nearly half. It was a secret that Daren had kept almost twenty years.

Here's Mud (or Something) in Your Eye

Daren and Jim often used that car to go to Tyler to the YMCA where they took Judo classes. One night as they were driving down the narrow farm to market road, they topped a small hill and were confronted with a small herd of cattle in the middle of the road. Daren dodged as many as he could before hitting one dead center of the hood, throwing it rump first into the windshield of the driver's side. The windshield shattered as the cow's rump penetrated the glass. The force of the blow caused the cow to expel a large portion of that day's digested grazings directly into Daren's face, covering it like a meringue pie in a food fight.

Though both were uninjured except for minor glass cuts, Jim feared for Daren's vision and told him not to blink. A school bus, on its way to a Junior High football game in Overton (in which Daren's little brother and I were playing), picked up the two boys and drove them to the hospital in Overton. It must have been a ridiculous sight as Daren got off the bus, his face still covered with a thick coating of cow manure.

Fortunately, Daren suffered no damage to his eyes, Dad's wise investment in insurance on the car covered the loss, and with his new car, he got his good gas mileage restored.

You Eat Watermelons, Too?

In the '50s and '60s farmers around here grew watermelons every summer. They were plentiful, they were cheap, and they were readily available through the midnight five-finger discount program. There is nothing sweeter than the heart of a "free" watermelon on a hot summer night. But when you got through with the watermelon there was always the problem of getting rid of the rind. No one wanted them in their trash can because the sweet smell attracted honeybees and wasps.

One good way to get rid of them was to jack up someone's car and put the rinds under the back wheels. When the person got in the car to go somewhere, the tires would spin loudly in the slick rind until it finally dug its way through to the ground. While this was a lot of fun, it was too labor intensive to be an effective way of getting rid of the rinds. Jim and Daren invented a far more exciting way of disposing of the rinds. Jim would get into the trunk of Daren's car with a box of rinds, then Daren would drive down the highway, often well above the speed limit, while Jim would drop the rinds out the back and listened to them skid along behind the speeding car.

Well, it worked for them, and one night it worked for me. Daren wanted to enjoy the process with Jim, but needed a driver so that he could get in the trunk; so on this rare occasion little brother was invited along. I did have a driver's license, and the prospect of driving one of the fastest hot rods in town was overwhelming. It was quite an experience driving a '56 Chevy with a bored engine, four speed transmission (in the floor), and a dump truck clutch. Jim and Daren had a ball sliding rinds and a couple whole watermelons, and I reaped the joy of my first time to drive ninety miles per hour.

He Finally Met His Match

As I mentioned earlier, Jim was very proud of the fact that in the four years he wrestled at the School for the Blind, he never lost a match by being pinned. With judo and karate training under his belt, he considered himself to be king of the hill. That was to change though when one day Dad and Jim were horsing around in the bedroom and Jim was intent on taking Dad to the mat. They scuffled for a while, then Jim made a lunge at Dad, but Dad sidestepped him and Jim crashed through the sheet rock wall between the studs and into the water heater closet, knocking the water heater over and breaking the pipes. Water went everywhere before Dad could go outside and get the water turned off. Jim was not hurt, but his pride did take a little nursing. The water heater had to be replaced and re-piped and the wall had to be repaired and repainted, but Jim learned a new respect for his elders that day.

Don't Limit Your Outlook

I am reminded of the story of the four blind men who encountered an elephant. Each of them felt of a different portion. The first felt of the tusk and thought an elephant to be like a spear. The second felt of the front leg and likened an elephant to a tree trunk. The third felt of the gigantic torso and thought the elephant to be like a wall. The fourth felt of the tail and marveled that the elephant must be like a rope. Each was correct in his individual observation, but none had seen the elephant.

If Jim had been one of the blind men, he would have petted the whole elephant and insisted on a ride.

— Chapter 10 —
The Things That Made Us Laugh

When every day of your life is a joyous occasion, you can find humor in every event, be it happy or tragic. So it was with Jim and me. We had totally optimistic outlooks on life. Every day was a new adventure; tomorrow was going to be even better. No matter what happened today, we could look back and see the humor of it tomorrow. Happy events were so much more pleasant to remember than pain.

An outlook like that didn't just happen. Our father, who loved to laugh and share his laughter, instilled it in us. He was always telling jokes and humorous stories. He was always setting up practical jokes on his friends. He collected jokes and cartoons and loved funny birthday and greeting cards. Most important of all, he understood humor; what made a story funny, how to set up a punch line and the importance of timing. Dad actually taught Jim and me these aspects of humor.

He never actually defined what made a joke funny, but taught us by example. I was almost forty five years old when I finally found a really good explanation of what makes something funny. I believe that I read somewhere that laughter is caused by the sudden and unexpected release of tension. The setup of a joke either builds toward tension or toward an expected and logical end. The punch line to the joke either releases that tension in an unexpected way or counteracts the normal logic that would take us to the end of the story.

FRITZ AND THE BLINK: AN OVERTURE TO LIFE

Our Twisted Humor

Our humor was tempered by the times in which we lived. With the imminent threat of nuclear war with the Russians being a constant item in the news, and later the space race with all its implications of global destruction, it was only natural that the humor of the late '50s and early '60s reflected the stress in the world at that time. Humor combated that stress by pointing out the ludicrous nature of such things as Assured Self-Destruction, Global Annihilation, Nuclear Winter or Viet Nam. Though your average Joe didn't spend more than a couple of seconds a day actually thinking about such things, comics, song writers, beatniks, hippies and cartoonists kept the subjects fresh on our minds with cruelty jokes, songs of protest, and political cartoons. Jay Leno wasn't around yet, but the Smother's Brothers, Stan Freberg, Brother Dave Gardner and many other entertainers were providing twisted views of the world situation, which we soaked up and regurgitated in volumes.

Mad Magazine was in its infancy. Alfred E. Newman adorned every cover with his freckles and buck-toothed grin. Each month we went to the Piggly Wiggly Store to buy the latest issue for only 25 cents. CHEAP! It was like getting the news of the last month, rehashed, twisted and perverted by some insane mind trying to wring the last drop of humor out of even the most tragic situation. Even the margins were filled with humor and cartoons.

TOM SWIFTY

Tom Swifties were the rage. These were statements followed by an adverb that punctuated the statement with its meaning. Examples:
"I am an incurable insomniac," he said sleepily.
"I got my wrist in a buzz saw," he said off handedly.
"I'm choking!" he cried breathlessly.
"I want to be a gymnast," she said flippantly.
"Why is your dog scratching so much?" he asked fleeingly.

"My name is Tonto," he said bravely.
"I don't worry about nuclear war," he said ashenly.
I think you get the point, but we could spend hours, re-stating the best and inventing new one-liner Tom Swifties.

Cruelty Jokes

Cruelty jokes were the rage for a few years around 1960. I think they were a relief from the tension we felt subconsciously about the possibility of nuclear war with Russia. A few examples:
Q. What do you call a leper in a hot tub? A. Stew

Q. If you meet a quadriplegic in the forest, what is his name? A. Stump

"But Mommy, I don't want to go to Europe!" "Shut up, kid, and swim."

"Mrs. Jones, can little Johnny come out and play baseball?"
"Now Timmy, you know little Johnny has no arms or legs."
"Yes, ma'am, but we need him for second base."

"Mommy, why is daddy running so fast?"
"Shut up, kid, and reload."

Little Johnny brought a beautiful electric motor to school for show and tell. It was chrome plated and when plugged in ran almost silently. "That is a marvelous motor," his teacher told him, "Where did you find it?"
"I got it off my brother's iron lung," replied Johnny.
"What did your brother say about that?"
"Uuuuuuuuuuuuuuuuuuuuuuuuh," replied little Johnny, simulating a person gasping for his last breath.

FRITZ AND THE BLINK: AN OVERTURE TO LIFE

There were endless variations of these jokes, the more ridiculous the better. We didn't think of them as cruel, only funny. They were politically incorrect; though the liberals had not sprung that ridiculous phrase on us yet. People could still laugh about what was humorous in this world without worrying that some small group of people would sue because it offended them to hear the truth expressed in such an outrageous manner.

Playing on Words

Another great type of joke was the play on words. This involved telling a story with a moral, similar to an Aesop's fable, but with the moral being composed of a convoluted version of a familiar moral with the words misplaced to fit the story. Examples:

A lunatic escaped from the funny farm and somehow made his way to Alaska where he would stalk the beach throwing rocks at the Arctic terns as they hunted for food in the sand. In his twisted mind, the tern was the root of all evil, and it was his obligation to rid the world of this threat. His quest was quite successful for it was no time at all until no tern was left un-stoned.

In a bloody war in the African bush, a tribal chief had his golden, diamond-incrusted throne stolen by a rival chief. To protect the throne, the rival chief hid it in the attic of his grass hut. One night, the throne fell through the grass floor of the attic and onto the bed of the rival chief, killing him instantly. Moral: If you live in a grass house, you shouldn't stow thrones.

The last example involves a concert pianist who discovered that his Steinway was out of tune. Because he was such a perfectionist, he wanted only the greatest piano tuner, a Dr. Oppernockity, to tune his piano so that it would be in perfect pitch. He summoned Dr. Oppernockity and had his piano tuned, after which he sat down to enjoy the sounds of a perfectly tuned instrument. As he played, he discovered that the third b-flat key above middle C was ever so slightly sharp. He went to his phone, called Dr. Oppernockity and requested that he return and re-tune his piano again to perfection. "I'm sorry, sir. I cannot come back," Dr Oppernockity explained, "For Oppernockity only tunes once!"

Then there was the Czechoslovakian midget who was trying to hide from the Gestapo during the German invasion of his country. He ran from house to house asking the occupants if they could cache a little Czech.

There was no end to the stories that could be dreamed up by the minds of that time along those lines.

Absolutely Pointless

Pointless jokes were the most fun of all. These were jokes that intentionally made absolutely no sense at all, but were used as part of a practical joke targeting one hapless victim. You had to have a group of people to help you, people who were instructed to laugh at the punch line (which didn't even remotely match the setup of the story) as if it were the funniest joke they had ever heard. The victim would see and hear everyone else laughing and begin to laugh too, never understanding what was so funny. The group's fake laughter would turn to real laughter as they watched the puzzled look and forced laughter of the victim who was trying to fit into the group. The final blow would come when you would ask the victim to explain what was so funny. Two such jokes come to mind:

There was a polar bear sitting on an iceberg. Suddenly, he stood up, put his paw on his head, turned around three times and said real slowly, "RADIO!"

The other was a riddle: You are riding down the street in your yellow canoe when one of your four, square wheels falls off. How many cookies does it take to make a gingerbread house? Answer: It is impossible because ice cream doesn't have bones.

FRITZ AND THE BLINK: AN OVERTURE TO LIFE

Jokes for the Gullible

Another type of joke required asking a question which in turn would evoke another question which only you could answer. We particularly liked these because there were generally two kinds of reactions to them. Either the person would catch the joke and feel stupid for asking the obviously trick question, or the person didn't catch the joke at all and felt stupid when it had to be explained to them that they had been set up.

For example, you could run up to a stranger and ask him, "What is the difference between an elephant and a henway?" Generally their response would be immediate and predictable.

"What's a henway?" they would ask.

"About three pounds," you reply.

Or

"What is the difference in a vase and a Grecian urn?"

"What's a Grecian urn?"

"About two bucks an hour."

Words of Wisdom?

The spin off of this was the statement that sounded logical but made no sense. Such as: "You can take a hotter shower sitting down because the water cools as it goes through the air." — Stan Freberg. George Carlin offered another version of this type of humor in a series of questions regarding the oddities of the English language. Such as:

"Why do they call them Hot Water Heaters? If the water is already hot, why heat it? Why do we drive on a parkway, and park in a driveway? Why is it called a hysterectomy when it is actually her-sterectomy? And why is it called a hernia when it usually is his-nea?"

Knock! Knock!

And there was the old reliable, the knock-knock Joke. Knock! Knock! — Who's there? — Banana — Banana who? — Banana, Banana— Knock! Knock! — Who's there? — Banana, Banana — Banana, Banana who? — Banana, Banana, Banana! — Knock! Knock! — Who's there? — Orange — Orange who? — Orange you glad I didn't say Banana??

Or better yet, run up to an unsuspecting person and tell them you have a new knock-knock joke. "You start it," you say. Not thinking, they reflexively blurt out, "Knock, knock."

Of course your next line is, "Who's there?" You can see the bright red letters I AM STUPID appear on their face as they realize they have been had.

Humor and Music Combined

Humorous songs of that era were much the same; they were humorous stories, put to music, often with truly outrageous sound effects. They were in all styles of music, jazz, rock, folk music, country, even spin-offs of classical music. No one style had a monopoly on humor; no popular song was safe from being mimicked. Jim used this to his advantage. He loved to play his guitar, sing, and entertain. Not only did he have the radio and new releases to work with; Mom and Dad had a treasury of pre-war 45 rpm records and Dad had a memory like an elephant for the lyrics of funny songs he had heard in the past. This gave us a range of more than thirty years of songs to choose from, many that most people our age had never heard.

One song, in particular, sticks in my mind. Dad would often sing us a song that went something like this: "I have tears in my ears from lying on my back in my bed while I cried over you." The picture that paints is outrageous, but Jim and I would sing that often when someone was looking for pity. I actually heard that song on the radio

FRITZ AND THE BLINK: AN OVERTURE TO LIFE

in 1972 as I pulled into the parking lot of the school where I was teaching at the time. I had never heard it on the radio before and have never heard it since, but it was a relief to know that Dad hadn't just made it up.

Other great songs of the day included "The Purple People Eater," "I Know an Old Woman Who Swallowed a Fly," "Ahab, the Arab," "The Witch Doctor," "My Boomerang Won't Come Back," and "Love Potion Number 9." For those of you old enough to remember those songs, I hope they still live in your minds as great treasures. Those of you who are too young, you don't know what you missed.

The one song that I most remember was sung by Stan Freberg and his orchestra and was in the archive of records my brother and I listened to. It is the only surviving 45-rpm record from that collection (many having been used for skeet shooting) and hangs proudly on the wall by my desk. It is probably too scratched to be enjoyed, but just seeing it there spawns fond memories of entertaining groups and shocking church parties when Jim or I would sing it. The song is called "Pass the Udder Udder." It is filled with wonderful dairy barn sound effects as well as hysterical lyrics and has a tune reminiscent of a country polka crossbred with a square dance. I wish I could get it played on some radio station, because I know it would be a comeback success. I haven't played that record in over thirty years, but still know the words by heart.

The song is about a ten-foot tall cow named Gladys who had one purple eye and twenty-seven "spigots." The brothers have to pass them back and forth to accomplish their milking chores and it really kept their hands full. The cow, though famous, claims she got her fame because of "pull."

Thank you, Stan Freberg, for the hours and hours of entertainment that this song provided and the memories it created. They just don't write them like that anymore. I wonder why? Jim once sang that song at a Baptist men's meeting. It raised a few eyebrows there, but we weren't kicked out of the church.

Parodies

Jim even created his own spin-offs of popular songs to entertain his friends. One such song was "I Walk the Line" by Johnny Cash. Jim's version was a little different and started like this:
I keep your memory in this heart of mine,
I keep my eyes wide open all the time,
I keep my pants up with a piece of twine,
Because you're mine, please, pull the twine.
My apologies go to the late Johnny Cash.

Folk Songs

Jim loved music and was an entertainer with his guitar and folk music. He loved the Kingston Trio, Peter, Paul and Mary, and the Smothers Brothers and had a whole repertoire of their music in his head that he could recall and sing at the drop of a hat along with other songs and ballads. One of his favorites was "Merry Minuet" by the Kingston Trio that parodied the tension of the nuclear stalemate of the time between the Soviet Union and the United States. It names off the groups that hate each other across the world, and concludes that someday, things will get out of hand, the atomic bomb will be used and "we will all be blown away."

It seems ironic now to look back on that song. We have lived through the arms race and the Cuban missile crisis and have seen the fall of the Soviet Union and the lessening of the threat of nuclear war. In 2002 we once again are faced with new threats of nuclear attack but from new enemies, the Chinese. Later in 2004 we feared the use of atomic weapons by the North Koreans. Now we don't seem to be able to laugh about it. At least in the '60s we didn't have a President who had given our enemies access to our technologies to improve their weapons systems to use against us. There are some things, I guess, that just aren't funny.

Conclusion

Laughter was the tie that bound us so close. Nothing was sacred, nothing was exempt from ridicule, but jokes were never used as weapons to belittle, only to uplift. Telling a fat joke to a fat person is not funny; it is insulting. We respected the feelings our friends and our enemies alike, but we could find humor in almost any situation and enjoyed it when we did. Because we learned our humor together from the same teacher, we knew intuitively what the other found funny in any situation we might happen upon. We could play off one another at the drop of a hat and did quite often as you will witness in the next chapter.

— Chapter 11 —
Pranks and Practical Jokes

My whole family was known for having a great sense of humor. Dad could tell a humorous story about almost any situation, profession or subject that came up in conversation. His humor was always clean, but funny and his timing would rival the best comedians of the day. Most impressively, his humor would be relative to the situation. He could use humor to break the ice with new people, to relieve stress, or just to put other people at ease. He was not being funny to impress any one or draw attention to himself, but it just flowed from him because he looked at life with joy and love in his heart. He was both victim and perpetrator of many practical jokes, and enjoyed either end of the spectrum equally. A well conceived "gotcha" was a work of art, even if he were made the goat.

My mother also had a great sense of humor, she loved to laugh, but she could not tell a joke. Her attempts at joke telling were funny because her timing was terrible and she often muffed the punch line. She learned early on that her best course of action was to ask Dad to tell a joke for her. Of course, Dad had a story to illustrate the problem.

A man decided he would join a joke club so he could enjoy hearing and telling jokes. The club met in a hall that resembled a church. The seats were like pews, but the book racks on the pews held joke books instead of hymnals. The person telling the joke would go to the podium, which resembled a pulpit. Instead of telling the joke, he would call out the number of the joke in the joke book and the "congregation" would read it and laugh. After several people had called out jokes and the members were sharing much laughter, the man decided it was time to try his hand.

FRITZ AND THE BLINK: AN OVERTURE TO LIFE

He made his way to the "pulpit," opened the joke book and called out, "Number 147." The members turned to the joke read it and just sat there without cracking a smile. "I'll try again," he thought to himself. "Number 283," he announced. Again the members read and again no reaction. He slammed the book on the podium and stormed back to his seat. "I never could tell a joke," he said to his neighbor.

Farewell to the Preacher

One of Dad's most memorable practical jokes involved our preacher who was moving to Berkley, California, to pastor a new church. The preacher had been a close friend of the family and we hated to see him leave. I was especially because he had a daughter my age of whom I was very fond. He came by the house for one last visit as he was leaving town to drive to California. Before leaving he asked Dad if he had anything for a headache. Dad went to the medicine cabinet and returned with a couple of pills. "Here, these should do the trick." The preacher took the pills and we said our farewells and watched sadly as they pulled away.

About two hours later, Dad received a phone call from Terrell, Texas, from a rather shaken preacher who had stopped to take a restroom break, only to find that his urine was bright red. Once his initial panic passed, he remembered the pills Dad had given him. Dad told him not to worry, the pills were kidney dye pills and he was perfectly all right. Several years later on a vacation to the west coast, we stayed in the preacher's home and the incident was still remembered, but with fondness.

Whether by heredity or environment, Jim and I also loved jokes and pranks. We would spend many hours sharing the latest jokes and laughing. We could find humor in almost any situation and were quick to jump on any opportunity to create pranks. "An idle mind is the Devil's workshop," it is said, but our two active young minds were a laboratory. We cooked up pranks with an enthusiasm that would rival the finest think tanks of M. I. T.

Living on a Higher Plane

After Jim moved back home to go to public school, he was too big to sleep in the same bed with his little brother anymore, so Dad closed in the garage and made Jim his own room. In front of his room was the carport, or more properly boat-port, because that is where the boat was parked for protection from the weather. Jim had his own door to the outside world, so his friends could come and go at will without having to come through the house and Jim could come home from his late-night outings with friends without disturbing the rest of the family who generally were asleep much earlier. It was also well enough separated from the main part of the house that the noise that was always generated by Jim and his friends did not disturb the rest of the household.

One Saturday night, Jim and I were up late in his room visiting, telling jokes, and laughing when we decided that we needed a change of scenery. It was in the fall of the year, and the night air was cool and fresh, so we decided that we would sleep outside on the flat roof of the carport where the ski boat was kept. We packed up our bedrolls, gathered snacks and drinks and were about to climb up on the roof when we realized that in the morning when the folks came to wake us up for church, they would need to know where we were. So we decided to leave them a note on the bed to let them know everything was all right.

Anyone else would have just left a note saying, *"We are sleeping on the roof of the carport,"* but not the Cohagen brothers. For us it was the perfect opportunity to leave a cryptic note, filled with clues. It was a treasure hunt, if you will. I don't remember the full content of that note, though my mother saved it for years, but it went something like this:

"Don't look for us in the house; we aren't there. We have decided to leave this earth and move on to a higher plane. We will no longer be able to ski on the lake, for we are above all that now."

We left the note on the bed and retired to the roof for the night.

The next morning we were awakened from our blissful slumber by Dad, standing on a stepladder with his head peering over the edge of the carport. "Wake up, guys. It's time to get ready for church."

We gathered up our things and climbed off the roof and went in the house where we were greeted by my mother's tear-filled eyes. She had thought we had been kidnapped! Dad, being the cooler head, figured we had only run away from home. Every closet door was opened from the frantic search of the house our folks had made. Our mother's red eyes continued to flow; though now they were tears of joy. She was so happy to see us home safe again that she forgot that she wanted to kill us.

Things That Go Boom in the Night

Jim had an electric guitar, which meant, of course, he had an amplifier. The family also had an old style reel-to-reel tape recorder that was used to record and playback lessons, and also for listening to books recorded by the Books for the Blind. It took little effort to link the two together so that we could record music and sounds and play them back with much greater volume. To that end one evening we decided to make a tape of sound effects. Pots and pans were great sources of bell sounds and squeaky door hinges sounded really spooky when amplified. Growling into the glass chimney of a kerosene lamp created a believable bear. Cups could be used on a table to make hoof beats. Wouldn't a little firecracker recorded and amplified sound like a huge bomb? The truth is it doesn't.

When an explosion occurs, the actual sound of the explosion only last a fraction of a second. It is the reverberation, or echo, that makes the audible, resounding boom we think of. If you record a firecracker on tape, especially with the poor quality of microphone we had available at the time, you only get a quick sharp bang with silence on either side. That was no good for sound effects. No one would believe that was an explosion.

The experimentation process began. How do you create a realistic, reproducible sound of an explosion? How do you stretch a millisecond bang into a five-second roar? Why not multiple bangs, linked together? But how could we do it? A nickel pack of fireworks did contain sixteen firecrackers with the fuses braided together. Why not light the whole thing and record that?

It was a slight improvement, but is still sounded like a series of short, sharp bangs rather than a continuous roar. There needed to be a way to fill in the spaces between the bangs. Again, reverberation was the key. Again, how do we make it happen?

What we really needed was an echo chamber, but on our limited budget, no budget, we had to improvise. Jim decided that confining the sound to a hollow space would help. The only hollow space available was a metal trashcan. What the heck, we had nothing to lose but another nickel pack of fireworks. Crank up the recorder. Light the fuse and throw them in the trashcan with the microphone. Cover the top with a board. Let nature take its course.

This time the results were much more favorable. The fireworks exploded closer together, the metallic reverberation helped fill in the gaps and we had our best recording of a controlled explosion, but it still was too shrill to sound like a big explosion. Our recording was a tenor and we needed a bass. The old reel-to-reel supplied the final solution. We had been recording at 15 feet per minute. But the recorder was a two speed. By playing back the recording at 7 1/2 feet per minute we doubled the length of the explosion and deepened its voice to a rich, throaty bass. The explosion lasted nearly five seconds and echoed beautifully. It was time to share our creation with the world, or at least the neighbors.

We took the recorder out to the carport, wired it to the amplifier with its twelve inch woofer, pointed the speaker up the street, away from the house, turned it on and let it rip. Not only did the recording echo, but the sound we produced also echoed off the houses up the street. It was beautiful, and bore repeating, several times.

Now did I forget to mention that all this had begun sometime around midnight, and that our parents were asleep on the other end of the house, four closed doors and four rooms away? Our folks were very sound sleepers, probably the result of having clear consciences and noisy kids. I don't think that even our carefully directed recordings of the explosion woke them up. It probably had more to do with the phone call they received from one of our neighbors up the street. At any rate, Dad suddenly appeared on the carport in his pajamas, eyes half open, suggesting that maybe it was a little past our bedtime and maybe we should GET IN BED!

Being obedient children, we halted our experiment and retired to Jim's bedroom, still reeking with the smell of flash powder, and settled down for a good night's sleep. It wasn't until the following afternoon when Dad got off work that we could share the results of our diligent efforts with him. Though impressed with the quality of our work, he did have a few choice words to share with us about our timing.

The Kidnapping

When it came to creating jokes and pranks, Jim and I had an advantage on most people. We had learned our humor together and knew each other so well, that we would often see the possibility for humor in a new situation and laugh together because we were both thinking the same thing, though it had not yet been said. We knew when the other was setting up a joke and could almost read each other's minds when it came to creating a humorous situation. The following story is the best example of our zest for the ridiculous. Jim was in college at the time, and I was a senior in high school.

One evening, a friend of mine and I had a double date planned. Since Jim had nothing better to do that evening, *he* decided he could come along with us. It was a cold winter day, by East Texas standards. It was probably around forty degrees, wet and windy. We rode around for a while, just visiting and talking, cracking jokes and enjoying life. We had chosen to ride around Kilgore for a while, just to see if anything was happening. This was THE BIG CITY, at least compared to Overton. The jokes got stale, the conversation boring. We decided something radical needed to be done to break the monotony.

Now at this time, I had my first car, a red 1966 Mustang with dual racing stripes from the front bumper to rear passing directly over the steering wheel. The stripes had been added to give the car its unique custom appearance. It also made it easy to spot since it was the only one of its kind in our area. The car was designed to carry only two comfortably in the front seat, though it had a back seat that could carry two more in relative comfort, if they didn't mind their knees under their chins. But that night we had Jim along as an extra and the back seat was more than a little crowded and uncomfortable.

My brother was a very talented person in many things such as music, speaking, debate, and mathematics. However, he excelled in one art that can only be appreciated in open spaces. He was a master of flatulence. That evening, with the assistance of a greasy cheeseburger from the Jersey Queen, he decided to produce his opus.

There was a basketball tournament going on at the high school gym. Not being great fans of the sport, we opted not to attend. However, we decided to drive by to see how the games were coming alone. When we arrived at the gym, one of my classmates was on the front porch. My friend rolled down the back window and called him over the car so we could discuss the scores. Just then Jim "Vesuvius" erupted! As the friend came close to the rear window to talk, he suddenly lost interest in discussing basketball and made a sudden retreat to the gymnasium, muttering something vile under his breath.

Keep in mind that it was a very cold night, making the necessity of rolling down all the windows until the symphony had run its course a tough choice. We could freeze to death or die of asphyxiation. Jim, who was oblivious to our peril, assured us that he would control himself the rest of the night.

Since Overton had no real entertainment of its own, we decided to go to Kilgore where there was much more night life. The twelve minute trip went well and the car began to recover from the ambiance. Just as we broke the plane of the city limits, Jim broke something else. This time it was far worse than the first.

My friend and I decided there was only one course of action to insure our survival. Jim would have to ride in the rumble seat. Since Mustangs did not have a rumble seat the trunk was the only logical alternative.

FRITZ AND THE BLINK: AN OVERTURE TO LIFE

I pulled my car into an almost deserted parking lot and my friend and I pulled Jim from the car, yelling and screaming at him, while pretending to beat him up. Though it had not been planned in advance, Jim almost instinctively and without explanation became part of the act, falling to the ground and moaning loudly. I opened the trunk and we unceremoniously threw Jim in. We were still yelling at our moaning victim as I slammed the trunk closed. We quickly jumped back into the car and I squealed the tires to make a rapid exit from the lot.

Remember that I told you that the parking lot was *almost* empty? Two men were parked on the other side of the lot, apparently discussing business, and witnessed the activities. For reasons unknown to me, they chose to jump in their cars and chase after us. Fortunately, my Mustang was lighter, quicker, and more agile than their Caddies were and it took only a few minutes to lose our pesky pursuers on the narrow streets of a black residential area.

The chase had been fun, but the escape was far more satisfying. The excitement and the laughter had made us all thirsty, so we decided to go to the A&W Root Beer Stand and get something to drink. A&W had carhops in those days and as we pulled in and parked under the canopy, we were met by a sweet young thing eager to take our order and get a tip. We ordered, "COKE," "COKE," "DR. PEPPER," "COKE," and she started to turn to go inside to fill our order.

"Wait!" I shouted. "We have one more order." She looked back in the window, a little puzzled by my request. She had four drinks ordered, and four people were in the car. "My brother is in the trunk," I explained. "He might want something." She looked a little bewildered as I got out from behind the wheel and walked back to the trunk and banged loudly on it with my fist. "You want something to drink?"

"Dogger Pebber," was the muffled reply from inside the trunk.

"What?" I yelled back.

"Dobber Pegger!" rattled from the trunk.

"Just a minute," I instructed the carhop. I got my key and unlocked the trunk. Immediately a hand flew out, then a leg. I shoved them frantically back in and slammed the trunk shut. I shouted at the lid, "Don't try that again or I'll never let you out!"

"OOOOH, Kaaaaay," was the sheepishly moaned response from the trunk.

Knowing that I now had the situation well under control, and knowing that Jim had picked up on the gag, I again unlocked the trunk and raised the lid open only a couple of inches. "Now, what do you want to drink?" I asked in a voice that expressed near anger. "A Dr. Pepper," Jim replied in a sheepish voice just before I slammed the trunk shut again.

The poor carhop was standing there; utter disbelief shown in her eyes and a certain amount of nervousness was apparent in her demeanor, but she wrote his order down on her pad. Before she went inside and called the cops, I felt an explanation was in order. With all the seriousness of a preacher at a wake, I told her the "truth."

"My brother was in a car wreck a while back," I explained. "He was cut up and burned pretty badly. He likes to get out of the house when we go places, but he looks so awful it embarrasses me to be seen in public with him."

I don't know exactly what emotion that carhop exhibited at that moment. I have never seen it before or since. There was a long silence before she slowly turned away and walked inside to fill our order. I got back into the car, with the windows up, of course, and retold the story to the other three. It was a miracle that the windows did not shatter from the roar of laughter that followed. When we saw the waitress inside approaching the door with our order, solemn faces were painted over our laughing forms. I rolled down my window and took the drinks as she handed them to me and passed them out to my passengers until only one remained on the tray. "I'll take that," I said as I took the drink and paid her. "Keep the change," I generously added.

She took her money, thanked me for the tip and had begun walking back to the door, but stayed outside as I got out of the car and unlocked the trunk. I opened it only enough to slip the cup in. "Here's your Dr. Pepper," a said rather roughly. I carefully handed the Dr.

Pepper to Jim, taking care to hide the contents of the trunk from her curious eyes.

"Thank you," Jim said from the trunk, in a voice so pitiful, it almost made *me* feel sorry for him. As I closed the lid, I could see the carhop still standing outside the door. She watched as I got back into the car, started the engine and pulled slowly away.

This had been so much fun, we wanted to keep it going all night, but A&W was the only place in town with carhops. So we drove downtown to find a place where we could let Jim out of the trunk. In the middle of downtown Kilgore, we were caught by a red light and as we sat patiently waiting for the light to change, who should pull up beside us on the right but a police car with two of Kilgore's finest inside. At that very moment, not knowing what was going on outside the car, Jim decided he had been in the trunk long enough. Still playing out the prank, he started banging on the trunk lid from the inside with his fist and yelling, "Help! Help! Somebody let me out! I'm being KIDNAPED!"

The decision I had to make next took only a fraction of a second, but in that fraction of a second I saw all the consequences of my situation flashed before my eyes, totally in focus and in TECHNICOLOR. I am in a car full of teenagers late at night, I have a blind kid in my trunk yelling "Kidnap," I have police glancing in my direction, and I have a brother who would swear he had never "SEEN" any of us before until after we had been fingerprinted and booked. I was going to be arrested, handcuffed and taken to jail. I was going to be humiliated beyond belief. I WAS GOING TO DIE!

Fortunately, it was winter, and policemen, who are really just people like us, only we didn't believe that at that time, get cold, too. They had their windows up and their heater on. So I told everyone to roll down the windows and at the same time I deftly grabbed the radio volume knob with the thumb and index finger of my right hand and twisted it full to the right, and began singing a Beach Boy's tune that was on the radio to the top of my lungs. Rhonda really helped me that night. The policeman behind the wheel gave us a long glance as the light turned green, and he pulled away. I guess I was fortunate that he didn't pull us over just to see what we were drinking, but fortunately the ploy had worked. As soon as the police car was out of sight, I opened the trunk and let Jim out.

I told Jim what had almost happened and Jim, of course, had a huge belly laugh about the police car, and agreed that he would have probably said exactly what I had thought he would. We laughed all the way home, and the story was told and retold for weeks. By the way, we NEVER did that again.

Mathematics and Figures

In Jim's high school class, there was one boy who many felt was rather effeminate; maybe it has something to do with the fact that his parents named him Sue. Actually, his name wasn't Sue, but it was just as bad, and maintains anonymity, so I will continue to refer to him as Sue. He later had his name changed to the more masculine sounding Cynthia, again not the actual name, but very much in line with the "masculine" name he chose. He was not a bad boy; in fact, he was actually very polite and quiet.

One day, Jim devised a prank, not so much to target Sue, but rather his math teacher, nicknamed "Thumbs" James to distinguish him from the principal who had the same last name, who was "Fingers" Floyd. Now the math teacher was a very reserved person, organized, polite, and almost shy. He was a very likeable person, and he was a very good teacher who enjoyed his job and his students. He was, however, at times very dull while teaching. I believe Jim sensed this and wanted to liven up the mood in the classroom.

At the front of the classroom was the blackboard, not chalkboard, but black slate. Above that were several teaching aids that hung like the old pull down maps used in the geography class. One had pictures of the different shapes studied in geometry, another had pie charts to demonstrate fractions, and one was a cloth blackboard with grids drawn on it for demonstrating graphing. At the time, the lessons were on graphs and charting, and Jim knew that the chart would be used in that day's lesson.

FRITZ AND THE BLINK: AN OVERTURE TO LIFE

This was the early '60s and *Playboy* had only recently made its debut, but most high school boys of the time were already familiar with the new concept of the "centerfold." Jim had one of his buddies bring the centerfold to school and between classes, while the teacher was in the lounge re-establishing his nicotine level before the next class, the friend taped the centerfold in the center of the pull down graph and rolled it back up. This was done without the knowledge of Sue, who had been intentionally detained in the hall by another conspirator.

The stage was set. All the students in the class, save one, were aware. The victim finally arrived, followed by the teacher, just before the bell sounded. Roll was called, and class began. Sometime during the class, one of the students asked Mr. Elliot to please explain one of the homework problems that involved graphing. Dutifully he explained the problem and then to demonstrate he pulled down the graphing aid, revealing Miss September (or some other equally inappropriate month) in all of her radiant glory.

The graph went back up immediately and the teacher turned to look at the students. All were solemn, save one. Sue, who was as surprised as the teacher, was snickering and giggling. Not taking time to think the situation through thoroughly, the flustered teacher grabbed the obviously guilty party by the ear and headed out the door toward the principal's office. Somewhere along the way he was stopped short as intellect overtook surprise and he realized that there was no way that this shy, sweet child would have pulled such a stunt. He returned to his classroom, apologizing to Sue for his outburst of unthinking anger, and never finished explaining the problem to the students. Jim told me that from that day on the pull-down graph was only used sparingly, and when it was used it was pulled down very slowly.

Dodge the Bottle

Somewhere along the way Jim developed a love of drinking, beer especially. I don't have much personal knowledge of this fact, because being the little brother I was never allowed to tag along on his nights out with his drinking friends. However, over the years, friends have related to me that he did indeed enjoy the buzz of booze and became somewhat overt under its influence. I mean how many people in their right minds would crawl into an oven and sit contentedly for an hour or so.

One story related to me, long after the fact, was about a game that Jim liked to play while riding around with one of his friends sucking down suds. I am told that he had a rather large thirst and capacity for the brew and the empty bottles soon became the source of entertainment. He would finish his drink and throw the empty bottle out of the window. Not so unusual in those days, I am told, but Jim did not throw the bottle out beside the road, or at road signs. He would throw the bottle forward in front of the car so that the driver would have to play "Dodge the Bottle" to avoid the broken glass and a flat tire.

One night Jim added a new and unexpected twist. He threw the bottle too high. It caught the resistance of the wind and slowed sufficiently to cause it to fall back on the car itself, more precisely, onto the windshield. The bottle shattered, but so did the windshield. It was the last time he got to play that game.

The Magic Car

Though Jim had nothing to do with this next story, I must include it because it was one of my personal best pranks. It involved a 1963 Falcon Futura that our family had. At the time, windshield washers were not standard equipment on most cars and because Dad used the car on the mail route on dusty back roads, he needed to be able to wash his windows while driving. He had an after market washer installed that had a pedal on the floorboard with a foot-powered pump to squirt water on the windshield and activate the wipers at the same time. Or by just tapping the pedal lightly, you could activate the wipers to wipe mist off the windshield without squirting water.

FRITZ AND THE BLINK: AN OVERTURE TO LIFE

My best friend, and dearest adversary, was a fellow named Clark. He and I were both proud of our intelligence, and were constantly struggling to out do each other; it was what made life and school interesting for us. One day he and I were riding around in the Falcon and just for fun I reached up to the dome light and simultaneously tapped the foot pedal to make the wipers clean the windshield.

Clark was surprised. "How did you do that?" he queried.

Not being one to miss an opportunity, I told him, "Somehow some wires got crossed when they were putting the car together. To turn on the wipers, you have to twist the dome light," and I dutifully demonstrated by reaching to the dome light and turning it while, unknown to him, I tapped the pedal again.

He fell for it, hook, line and sinker. I went back to my driving, but watched from the corner of my eye as he reached up to the dome light and gave it a twist. Again I tapped the pedal to match his twist and the wipers came on at his command. "Gotcha!" The ploy was sweet and complete, and for years Clark would tell friends about that incident.

It wasn't until nearly thirty-five years later that I finally told him the truth, and the look on his face was worth all the years I had waited.

Just a Dog!

There was a joke in *Reader's Digest* that almost cost us our lives. I will not tell the joke, though you can probably reconstruct it from the story.

One day we were going to go to Kilgore, for what I do not remember, but we were riding with our grandfather in his 1956 Buick Road Master. We had stopped at a highway intersection where it was difficult to see the traffic on the crossing highway. Jim and I were sitting in the back seat. Seat belts were not the law then so we were not buckled in. Papaw asked Dad if there was anything coming. His reply was part of the joke that I referred to earlier. "Only a dog," he said. Papaw eased down on the gas to pull out on the road. Dad lunged across the car from the passenger's seat and threw the automatic transmission into park. The big car lurched to a sudden stop just as a Greyhound Bus flew by, only inches from our front bumper.

Going Too Far

It sort of reminds me of the old story Dad used to tell about the man who stole a friend's pig. He was caught and taken to the judge. "I only took it as a joke," he explained to the judge.

The judge asked him, "How far do you live from your friend?"

"Only about three miles," he replied.

"Guilty!" proclaimed the judge.

"But, your Honor, I told you, I only carried the pig off as a joke," the man cried.

"Well, sir, I think you carried the joke a little too far."

And so it was with us; we loved jokes and pranks, but we tried not to carry them too far.

— Chapter 12 —
Skis, Sleds and Scooters
Motion Was the Name of the Game

It didn't matter if it were a tub, a pool, a creek, a lake or an ocean, water was water and Jim and I loved it. A bath tub was as good as an ocean for splashing, though not in the eyes of our parents who had to mop the bathroom floor on many occasions. We both learned to swim at very early ages, and we enjoyed swimming below the surface as much as swimming on top. This kept Mom on her toes when we went to the pool, because she never knew for sure if we were drowning or just just trying to set a new breath-holding record.

Jim and I were both good swimmers. We both earned our lifesaving merit badges through Boy Scouts, and loved to swim in pools, lakes or anywhere else there was enough water to cover our heads. Boating, however, was a rich man's sport and we were first introduced to the fun of being dragged across the water on a vacation to De Pere, Wisconsin one summer to visit one of Dad's old army buddies. The family had a lake house and a boat and seven kids, and we were invited to go with them and learn to aquaplane. An aquaplane is like a toboggan pulled behind a boat. You sit on it and hold onto a rope tied to the front of the thing and the boat pulls you up on top of the water. By leaning you can steer to a limited degree. It was fun as a first experience, and we kept the memories of that trip for years.

A few years later, a friend of Dad's bought a ski boat and since his wife did not like to drive it, Dad was invited on the ski trips so that his friend could ski with his family. Of course, our family was always invited and never refused a ski trip. Jim and I learned to ski on Lake Tyler behind a Red Fish ski boat with a thirty-horsepower motor.

Jim and I took to skiing like ducks to water and after only about three attempts we were both skiing.

Our Family Obsession

In 1960 Dad decided we needed a ski boat. Dad's excuse was Mother's Day. He decided the boat would be Mom's gift, and she awoke that morning to find a new ski boat sitting in the driveway with a huge ribbon on it. Dad was such a romantic; he often gave gifts for the family to Mom on special occasions.

For the next six years, our family was at the lake at least four days a week when the weather was warm enough to ski. Dad had an air horn and would give Jim directions with a code they devised. He could let Jim know when it was safe to go outside the wake, when to fall in behind the boat and when to swing right and let go so that he could end up near the beach.

Our first outboard motor was too small and could only pull two skiers. That lasted only a season and was quickly replaced with a seventy-five-horsepower motor, which on one occasion pulled five skiers at one time. It was also much faster and more fun to ski behind. Jim and I became accomplished skiers and often skied together, crossing each other's paths and attempting other tricks. It was inevitable that we would have to do stunts together. We both could slalom, that is ski on only one ski, so it was only logical that if two people could ski on two skis separately, then two people could ski on two skis even though only one person was wearing them both.

Our first attempts at double skiing were with me clinging onto Jim's back as the boat pulled both of us out of the water on his skis. This did have some drawbacks. First, my added weight caused a considerable strain on his arms, since he had to hang onto the rope alone as we were both being pulled onto the water. Also, from time to time, the rush of the water over and around our bodies would be stronger that I could resist and I would be pulled off before we could get up. On one occasion, trying not to fall off, I dug my claws (both hands) into his shoulders and back and left a pair of tracks that looked like he had been attacked from behind by an angry tiger. It was then that we decided there had to be a better way.

Our new approach was for both of us to get up on the surface, he wearing two skis and me only one. I then would approach his left side and carefully step on to his right ski with my free right foot, then step out of my slalom ski and step on the back of his left ski. This was much easier, and preserved the skin on his shoulders. Next, Jim would bend at his knees and I would step on his thigh and climb to his shoulders and sit for the remainder of the ride. We must have been quite a sight.

As we got older, Jim and I were free to take the boat to the lake with our friends, much the same as we were able to use the family cars whenever we needed them. Daren and Mitch often went on ski outings to drive the boat and ski with us. On occasions, Jim even drove the boat when the lake was not crowded. He would sit behind the wheel, and a friend or I would sit in the passenger's seat and give directions. When the lake was empty, Jim could cutup and steer for long distances before we approached land. He loved the thrill of speed, wind blowing in his face, and the g-forces generated by quick, sharp turns. I mean, after all, if you can drive a truck then you can drive a boat. Besides, there was far less chance of running into anything in the middle of a large lake.

Skiing, Louisiana Style

Our uncle Cecil, who lived in Louisiana, outside of New Orleans, also liked to ski. His boat had a 110 hp Mercury engine and was much faster than anything we had ever skied behind. On one visit to his home, we were invited to go skiing, an opportunity we could not pass up. In southern Louisiana, skiing is not always done on a lake, as we were to soon learn. We launched the boat into one of the bayous a few miles from his home.

A bayou in southern Louisiana had a few new features that we had never encountered in Lake Tyler. The sides of the bayou were lined with cypress trees, complete with cypress knees that stuck out of the water like teeth ready to bite. This precluded landing on the bank, so all skiing was done from the center of the bayou. Second, the water is teeming with needle-nosed gar that often rose to the surface and leisurely rolled their bodies on the surface before diving down again. You found yourself constantly eyeing the water in front of you, looking for these scaly mines, and dodging them as they appeared, a problem that did not concern Jim in the least. Also in the back of your mind as you ski along is the occasional alligator or water moccasin you might encounter. But the biggest surprise was something encountered while as I was skiing. We rounded a bend in the bayou and found ourselves coming face to face with a tugboat pushing a large barge up stream.

In a lake with other ski boats, you get accustomed to jumping the waves created by other boats, but a barge creates a wake about six feet high. I knew I could be in trouble when the ski boat topped the wake and disappeared behind it. A few seconds later, I was face to face with a six-foot wall of water. I gripped the handles with all my might and hung on for dear life as I rose suddenly up this mountain of water. I was amazed how smooth the transition from flat to slope was, but amazement changed to panic as I reached the crest and continued upward as the back of the wave fell away, sending me to about twelve feet above the water. My landing was less than graceful, but I survived and stayed on my skis.

Once again on smooth water, I signaled to Uncle Cecil to go faster and he was happy to oblige. His boat would do about forty-five miles per hour, a full fifteen miles per hour faster than I had ever skied before. I cut back and forth, and as I crossed the wake and swung to the right, Uncle Cecil decided to cut hard left and reverse his direction. Like a rock in a slingshot, the circular motion increased my speed and I was thrown to the full length of the rope on the right side of the boat's path. I was precariously close to the cypress knees along the edge of the bayou. I guessed my speed to be approaching sixty miles per hour and the cypress knees were blurry as they passed by so closely. I kept thinking to myself, "If I fall here, I will surely die, impaled on a cypress knee, and the alligators will have me for lunch." I guess it was that thought that kept me from falling until I had managed to gain some clearance from the shallow water and cypress knees. When I did fall I was still near the sixty miles per hour speed and bounced three or four times like a rock skipped on a pond, then slid on top of the water for about fifty feet until my speed slowed enough to let me sink into the water. That was enough for me.

Jim, having only heard the description of my near death and fall from those in the boat who did not share my point of view of that experience, joyfully jumped in the water and took his turn with the alligators and gars, totally unafraid of what he could not see. His ride was much tamer than mine was, though he did hit a gar as it was rolling on the surface and got knocked off his skis. This had little effect on Jim's enjoyment of the trip and he figured that the gar had gotten the worst end of the deal anyway.

That skiing trip left indelible memories. Several years later, when Lyndon Johnson was President, there was a joke that brought that experience back clearly in my memory. It seems that in his fight for civil rights, President Johnson had taken a tour of the South to see the conditions there. As he was flying over Louisiana in Marine One, the presidential helicopter, he saw a ski boat with two Cajuns pulling a black man on skis. He ordered his pilot to land so he could congratulate those men on their contribution to easing the racial tensions in that area by their obvious example of fellowship between the races. He landed, waved the boat over to the bank, and gave the two Cajuns in the boat his best political speech on the merits of brotherhood and civil rights. He immediately got back in Marine One and flew out of sight.

The two Cajuns sat in their boat dumbfounded. Finally, one asked, "Who the heck was that?"

"I don't know," replied the other, "but he sure don't know much about trolling for alligators."

Every time I recall skiing on the bayou, I wonder if Uncle Cecil was disappointed that he didn't catch any alligators that day.

Timing Is Everything

It was the summer of 1965, Jim was home from college and I was attending a National Science Foundation summer program at Texas A&M University. Mom, Dad, Jim and some of his friends had gone to the lake to ski. The day had been delightful, and Jim was skiing. When it came time to return to the beach, Dad made his usual approach and signaled Jim with the air horn to swing right in preparation for the left turn that would take him to the beach. Jim crossed the wake and pulled to the right as Dad turned left toward the beach. Suddenly, a boat that Dad had not seen was bearing down on our ski boat and Dad had to dodge it and was momentarily distracted. Jim in the meantime continued to pull to the right, approaching the shore rapidly. Dad quickly sounded the horn, the signal for Jim to let go of the rope and coast into the shallow water near the shore. Unfortunately, the signal was a little too late for Jim, who was already very near to the shore and still at full speed. Seconds later, Jim's skis hit the bank and he did several cartwheels and assorted flips on the beach. Thanks to his fine physical conditioning and judo training that had taught him how to roll when he took a fall, Jim was able to tumble and roll to absorb some of the shock. Our family physician, Dr. Jim, was skiing with the family that day, and remembered that Jim was "pretty shook up," but not hurt seriously. "He certainly gave us a scare," he recalled.

Dad was still pretty shook when he called that evening to tell me about the incident, but by the time I came home from Texas A&M Jim's bruises and scrapes were almost healed and the incident was the subject of much humorous joking. Skiing was not taken off the list of great pastimes, though in the future more attention was given to the landings.

I got to hear several versions of the tale from Mom, Dad, Jim and the other friends who were there. Each one was different, but none pointed blame at any party for what had happened; it was just an accident and another incredible story in Jim's charmed life. It scares me to think what might have happened if that same incident had happened today. Some social worker would come take Jim out of the family and Dad would be in jail for endangerment of a child, even though Jim was twenty years old at the time.

Frozen Water Is As Much Fun As the Liquid

Winters are generally mild in East Texas and snow, I mean a real snow that sticks to the ground and accumulates to more than two inches, only happens every five to seven years. Sleet and freezing rain occur much more often, usually at least one time each winter. But for kids, ice is ice, and you take advantage of the fact that it is on the ground. Since schools here generally closed for ice, you had the time to enjoy it.

When snow or ice occurred, kids ran to the garage to find anything that would provide the means for a good slide; plywood, cardboard boxes, shovels, wooden ladders, or if you were lucky enough to have a metal trash can lid with the handle removed, you had it made. No one owned a pair of snow skis in East Texas and I only saw one real Flexible Flyer sled with steel runners, but that didn't stop anyone.

The other problem was that East Texas has gentle rolling hills, and there were very few of them large enough or steep enough to afford a good slide of more than about fifty feet. Brandon Hill, which was only a few blocks from the house, was an exception. So when the ice came, kids gathered there to slide before the cars tore ruts in the sleet and ice and destroyed the good sliding conditions.

Jim and I were no different than any of the other kids in our town. We relished the joy of a good slide as much or more than anyone did. Jim especially enjoyed the rush of the wind, the sound of the ice sliding below whatever we were on, and the occasional surprise ending of the ride in a ditch, in a clump of bushes, or pinned under a parked car on the side of the road.

Sleds with Multiple Seats

On several occasions, we would take the old wooden ladder out and be towed around town behind Dad's car on the icy streets. If you had horsepower to make you go; you didn't need a hill. Unlike snow, if you fell off the ladder onto sleet and glazed ice, it was not a soft landing, but padded by several layers of warm clothing, it never hurt much. However, when we slid off the side of the road into a water-filled ditch with the temperature well below freezing, a hasty retreat to the house for a warm shower and dry clothes was in order.

Have Scooter — Will Travel

When you became a teenager you yearned for motion, acceleration, wind in your face and freedom to go. It didn't matter so much where, just that you could go. At age 13 I got a Cushman Highlander motor scooter and a license to drive it. At the time, I was a freshman in high school and Jim was a senior. A whole new world of freedom opened up to us. We both loved the noisy ride, it sounded like we were going much faster than we were, especially after I exchanged the standard muffler for a chrome plated Eagle exhaust pipe and gutted the baffles from inside.

Good roads, bad roads, no roads, it didn't make any difference. Bumps just added to the joy of going places. Jim loved to sit on the back and exert a certain amount of directional control by leaning his body side to side. This made riding with him a rather treacherous undertaking. Sometimes he would lean when it was totally unexpected; causing the scooter to swerve in a direction I really didn't wish to go. This was especially dangerous when I was meeting oncoming traffic. Jim didn't care. It was his job to provide the excitement, mine to save our lives. I guess we both enjoyed the thrill, though looking back I know God must have been a third passenger on several occasions.

This fun only lasted about a year until I got my operator's license to drive a car when I was fourteen, and joined the ranks of reckless teenage drivers that was so prevalent in those days. Though Jim and I never had a wreck when we were together, it was not for lack of trying. I was quite reckless, even wild some say, when behind the wheel of a car, but I just thought of it as testing the limits of performance of the car and myself.

— Chapter 13 —
Jim's College Years

High school was over and Jim had completed his overture to life. He was ready to move onward and upward toward act one of his opus. His optimism and expectations overshadowed any fears or anxieties he may have had. In the conclusion of his autobiography he expressed his anticipation of the years ahead.

"The materials found in this book serve as an overture to my life, for just as the overture of an opera sets the general mood for the performance to follow, so the events and persons described in this (his) *book have served to shape my beliefs and way of thinking."*

Later he continues to express his vibrant optimism for what life has in store for him in the future.

"Now that the overture is finished, it should be interesting to see how the rest of the performance turns out; with the basic themes such as have been presented in this overture, it should also be a real challenge to attempt to maintain them throughout the rest of the show. However, if what is yet to come in my life is as rewarding as has been its overture, then ON WITH THE SHOW!"

Kilgore Junior College

Jim had a great future ahead, and as we say here in East Texas. He was ready to move onto college and the independence it promised him. He was already speaking Spanish and French, studying Esperanto, an artificial language that was supposed to be adopted by the UN as the universal language of that body. He moved on to

FRITZ AND THE BLINK: AN OVERTURE TO LIFE

Kilgore Junior. College to get his pre-requisite courses behind him, make new friends, and prepare for Baylor University, where he hoped to study law or political science. His ultimate goal was to learn a couple of more languages and join the diplomatic corps as an interpreter, preferably in South or Central America. The cold war was in full swing, so German was his choice for a fourth foreign language, followed by Russian.

Kilgore Jr. College had a trades program for the handicapped that taught watch repair and jewelry making, but Jim wasn't into being taught how to be handicapped. However, he did find many friends among the students there. Jim had friends with no legs. He pushed the wheelchair; they guided the direction. He had friends with no arms. He carried things as they walked with him. He met friends who were mutes. He had learned signing in the past. He met midgets or dwarfs and they stood as tall as John Wayne did in his mind. If he had what his friend lacked, they shared and both benefitted. If they wanted to complain about their disability, he left them behind. Pity was the one handicap that Jim could not abide.

Jim had a mind like a sponge. He remembered everything he heard, felt, and experienced and could recall and process ideas like a computer. Jr. College was a breeze, and Jim spent as much time developing relationships as he did studying. He claimed to be members in two local fraternities, I Felta Delta and Phi Tappa Kegga. He loved to tell people that sex education by Braille was the greatest course he took there. He was active in the Baptist Student Union and spent hours there singing and playing his guitar with his friend Carl.

Carl recounted a story about one day when he and Jim were walking to the mailbox to send some letters. Jim dropped one of his letters and after a few steps realized that it had fallen. Carl offered to go back and get it off the ground, but Jim insisted he would do it. "He turned on his heels, walked back ten or twelve feet, bent down and put his hand right on the letter," Carl recalled. "I asked him how he did that."

As Jim walked back to join Carl, he thought a second then replied matter-of-factly, "I don't know."

Another incident Carl loved to tell about occurred in German Class. His professor was a large Norwegian who had come to the United States after World War II. Jim already spoke German quite well, having studied it in high school with tapes and records. Sometimes when he would get bored with the lesson, Jim would doze off. On one particular occasion, Jim not only dozed off, but also began snoring loudly. The professor walked over to Jim's desk, shook him by the shoulder until he awoke and then told him, "Jim, I can't always tell when you are awake or asleep, but, please, don't snore."

Tripping the Blind Boy

There was a bus that came to Overton to carry college students to Kilgore and Jim rode the bus daily to classes. He settled into his studies and was a member of the Baptist Student Union, the BSU as it was called, or as he referred to it "the Bijou." It was here that he met a young lady who he called "Kat." For the next two years she would be one of his best friends, though never girlfriend. "Kat" was a very sweet, congenial and pretty girl. She was also very large. To my best recollection, from my then five foot three inch frame, she stood somewhere over six feet and two inches. This was of no consequence except that it did set up one of Jim's favorite stories about "Kat."

Being friends, and Jim being a gentleman, he would often carry her books, and his, as they walked on the campus. The sidewalks between the administration building and the BSU were old and had cracked leaving the surface uneven in many places with several spots where one section had risen above the next by an inch or more. This presented the possibility of a tripping accident to anyone who could not see the cracks.

On one occasion, as "Kat" and Jim were walking, he found one of those spots, and being a true follower of the Law of Gravity, Jim found himself sprawled on the concrete with text books scattered all around him. Not wishing to appear clumsy or worse yet blind, he instinctively knew how to handle the situation. "Why did you have to trip me?!" he bellowed loudly enough for anyone within sight range of the incident to hear. "Kat," of course, was embarrassed beyond words, and had to swallow all pride. Jim was pleased at himself for saving face. Kat helped Jim up, gathered up the books, and swore an oath to kill Jim for embarrassing her so completely. But you know; she never did.

Baylor University and Independence

After two years of intense playing around and some study, Jim graduated from Jr. College as Salutatorian and prepared to go to Baylor. He once told a reporter who was doing a story about him that the reason he was salutatorian was that he *"had done a little too much playing around, I guess."* He stayed home that summer, enjoying his old hometown and college buddies. That fall he moved to the Dunn House, an apartment house about three blocks from the Baylor campus. He immediately made friends who helped him get oriented and walked with him to class a couple of times until he had a map in his mind of where his classes were. After that, he walked alone to class every day; he didn't wish anyone to be inconvenienced having to watch out for him.

I found an old article about Jim's life at Baylor, written in *The Baylor Lariat,* Baylor's Student Newspaper, dated February 5, 1966. The text of that article is included in hopes that it will be as interesting to you as it was to me when I found it among some of my dad's things in September of 2002.

>   For Junior Jim Cohagen Studies, Walk Home
>   Presents No Problem
>   by Tommy Kennedy, *Lariat* Staff Writer

>   Jim Cohagen strolled unaccompanied past Collins Hall, traipsed across the Pat Neff mall and walked to his Dunn House apartment at 1615 South Fifth Street.

He and a friend chartered the tricky sidewalks of the mall last September. Now he usually takes the shortest route to his destination and seldom meets any problems after the green light at Fifth Street signals him that it is safe to cross Speight Avenue.

"I do wish they'd move those trash cans by the drug store," he said. Then he added, "They're not much of a problem any more. I've about got them figured out."

When he reaches Dunn House Cohagen, a junior political science major from Overton, begins to study. "Most of my texts are on tape word for word. I've gotten to where I can turn my tapes up to double speed and still understand," he added. "But listening to a recording playing that rapidly requires fast thinking and accurate thinking," he said.

In class he doesn't ordinarily take notes. "I miss out on the lecture," he explained. Occasionally, though, he uses a special stylus to write lecture thoughts in Braille on notebook paper backed by a mat.

The system worked well enough for a 3.4 grade point average the first semester.

Cohagen types most of his tests but sometimes takes oral examinations. "I learned to write my name once but I had to think too hard to write," he said." The first time I handed a check to the lady at the drug store, she said it looked like Greek."

In his spare time Cohagen listens to friends read books, magazines and newspapers, including the comics. His favorites are *B.C.* and *The Wizard of ID.*

Other hobbies include playing the guitar, listening to music and attending shows or sports events. "I go to shows all the time, but usually not by myself," Cohagen said. "You can tell a lot about what's happening by the music and dialogue."

Cohagen receives *Readers Digest* written completely in Braille and *News Week* 45-rpm records. "There are no advertisements in the *Digest* and the book section is always included."

Cohagen finds time to attend major competitive sport events. At football games he listens to the commentary and simultaneously hears the crowd's reaction. As for basketball, "Nobody can describe it better than radio announcers."

Cohagen wrestled and practiced judo in his earlier years. Now studies keep him too busy for these activities.

The junior remembers acquaintances by the sound of their voices. "Everyone has a different voice," he said. "I've never heard two people talk exactly alike."

Sometimes Cohagen senses certain persons by their footfalls and even determines two personal characteristics by merely shaking hands. The height of the person and the type of work he does, Cohagen judges by instinct.

How high he reaches to shake a hand or the level he reaches indicates one's height to Cohagen. A tough or callused hand indicates a manual laborer while a soft hand usually means he is meeting a professional person.

Cohagen guessed this writer's height within one inch and correctly stated he, the reporter, has done no recent manual labor.

The Cohagen philosophy ranges from thoughts about long, girlish hair on boys to the resumption of bombing North Viet Nam.

"I think if a group wears their hair like that and somebody wants to copy them out of admiration, it doesn't bother me," Cohagen said. "They'll grow up."

On bombing North Viet Nam Cohagen said, "I think when you fight a war you should fight to win it, not to maintain it. Of course, I'm not as experienced in these things as (politicians and military men) are. "It's easy to sit around and debate these things but not making the decisions."

Cohagen transferred to Baylor from Kilgore Jr. College. As a political science major he would like to find work somewhere in Latin America, a place he has enjoyed visiting many times, or go into teaching.

Thus far his first year has been most rewarding. "As far as I'm concerned, Baylor people, on the whole, are some of the finest people around."

I'd Rather Do It Myself

Jim made friends quickly anywhere he went. He had no fears about new places because he knew that there would be people wherever he went whom he could learn to like and who would like him in return. He would not let himself be a burden to someone who might be trying to help him and had a sense about him that told him when he was.

In another article in the *Baylor Lariat*, Mr. Lucy Dunn, owner of Jim's apartment house recalled: *"I remember one day he asked me to set up the ironing board for him. 'I'll iron the shirts for you,' I said.*

"He said, 'No, my mother would skin me alive.'"

This was Jim's polite way of saying, "I have to do these things myself, as I will have to do them for the rest of my life." Jim was rarely rude with his refusals to accept help, but he was consistent. If he were going to a new place, where he didn't know the layout and knew he would have to accept help. If someone who was not familiar with his ability then offered to lead him somewhere, he would accept that help with one strict guideline: "I will hold on to your arm; you will not hold mine."

This is a lesson I would pass on to any sighted person who reads this story. When the opportunity comes for you to help or assist a blind or handicapped person, don't be offended if they do not readily accept your methods and give you instructions as to how you can best help them. Remember that they are individuals, generally very independent, and you are the intruder into their struggle to maintain the style of living they have built for themselves. They have their preferred methods of doing things, so respect their feelings and methods.

— Chapter 14 —
A Tribute to Friends

For reasons of privacy most of the names of Jim's friends used in this book are all first names only, though they probably wouldn't mind their names being associated with the story, They, of course, will recognize themselves in the stories and by their descriptions here, and I hope they find that my memory of them is accurate.

From the time Jim decided to return home to attend public school, he was fortunate to develop a number of very good friendships that made it possible for him to expand his universe immensely. In a town as small as ours, with a school that had only about a hundred students in the top six grades, Jim found an amazing variety of friends, most of whom you have met in previous chapters. I will not give their full names, but they know who they are and if they read this tribute, I hope they will accept my deepest appreciation for the parts they played, individually and collectively, in the development of Jim's world. Each of these friends had very different personalities, and for the most part did not regularly associate with each other except through the contact they shared with Jim. However, each friend provided a particular relationship with Jim that fulfilled certain specific needs he had. He, in turn, gave each of them memories of growing up with a special friend that will last a lifetime. The one thing they all had in common was their acceptance of Jim's lack of sight as nothing special. Many of the names have been changed to protect "the innocent."

FRITZ AND THE BLINK: AN OVERTURE TO LIFE

Daren

First and foremost was Daren. I guess Daren was Jim's most special high school friend. They shared a love of speed, mischief, judo, and jokes. Daren was constantly working on his car. No car ever had enough power, a loud enough muffler, or fast enough take-off. The phrase "Bat-out-of-Hell" really doesn't do his driving justice. Pedal-to-the-Metal had not been coined yet, but would have been more descriptive of his driving habits. Smoking tires on takeoffs, squealing tires sliding around corners, and landscapes passing the windows as a blur were all part of the experience of riding with him. In spite of all that, he was a very good driver who knew the exact capabilities of his car and stayed just inside of them. I still believe to this day that Daren was one of the best drivers I have ever known.

Daren was always working on his cars, experimenting with ways to get more power and speed. He once came up with a mixture of kerosene and mothballs which was supposed to add horsepower, but basically it only caused clouds of white smoke to blow from the exhaust like a mosquito fogger. He claimed that one of his cars was so well known by the Highway Patrol, that they would stop him on sight. He joked that he needed a large pair of sunglasses to put on the car to disguise it.

Daren was quite rotund, which lead to his high school nickname, Hippo. Daren did not like that nickname, so Jim shortened it to Hip to remove some of the stigma. For his size, Daren was quite agile and flexible, and he and Jim wrestled and carried on like brothers. Daren was a regular on the family water skiing outings, though it was quite a tug getting him on top of the water. He eventually solved that problem by building his own personal oversized water skis.

Jim and Daren also shared a love of judo, wrestling, and Karate. They would spend hours in the backyard throwing each other around and practicing kicking and punching and tying each other in knots. They took Judo and Karate classes together in Tyler at the YMCA. When they were not beating up on each other, they would be skiing on the lake, riding around thinking up mischief, or just sitting around telling jokes one after the other. After high school Daren got married and these best of friends quickly diverged to different life styles.

Mitch

Mitch was a tiny guy. He had a chiseled face, an eagle beak and an East Texas accent that would rival the worst attempts of Hollywood actors to talk like Texans. He and Jim looked like Mutt and Jeff, but a common love of music, jokes, and mischief bound them together like brothers. Mitch's family couldn't afford to provide him with a car of his own, but Dad always had a car available for Jim's friends to use when they wanted to go somewhere, and Dad did keep good insurance on his vehicles. There wasn't anything Jim could think of that Mitch wouldn't do with him. Many were the nights that our house rang with the sound of guitar music and singing from those two.

Mitch wouldn't pull any punches with Jim. He admitted to me that he took great pleasure in trying to run Jim into parked cars while they were walking down the street. This was not as easy as it sounds, since Jim could hear the echoes of their voices and footsteps off the cars and know they were there. Mitch, however, surmised that if he could get Jim distracted or laughing he could "jam his radar" so to speak. So he would crack jokes and exchange insults in order to get Jim off guard then get Jim to chase him while distracted. He still laughs today about the loud thud Jim would make as he ran into the hood of a parked car. The only problem was, and Mitch discovered this as I had long years ago, Jim would get right back up and keep coming, and you had better be able to stay out of his reach until he cooled off, or you would become the victim of Jim's revenge.

FRITZ AND THE BLINK: AN OVERTURE TO LIFE

Carl

In college, Jim met other friends. Carl was his intellectual buddy and fellow musician. Carl is now a successful lawyer in a neighboring town. I never knew exactly what they did together, for most of the time they were locked in Jim's room studying or making music. They did form a small folk-singing group and entertained around the area and at the Baptist Student Union. About the only association I had with them together was at the dinner table; they both loved to eat. Carl was especially fond of Mom's soft-shell tacos that were a staple at our house. He could inhale them as fast as Mom could make them. He told me once that his personal record was sixteen tacos at one sitting.

Dad would joke with Carl about claiming him as a dependent on his income tax forms since he had to feed him so much. Carl told me that his dad said the same thing about Jim. Carl has remained a friend of the family for many years, and remains a friend of mine to this day.

When I told Carl I was writing this book, he told me stories about Jim that I had never heard before. Jim spent about as much at Carl's house as Carl did ours, and Carl was amazed at how Jim could walk anywhere in his house without running into furniture or walls. One night, Jim and Carl came into the house rather late, and all the lights were off. The light switch was on the opposite side of the den, so Carl told Jim to wait while he crossed the room and turned on the light. Jim told Carl just to put his hand on his shoulder and follow him through the room since he didn't need lights anyway. What neither one of them knew was that earlier that night Carl's mother had rearranged the furniture in the den. Very soon, Jim found himself lying face down on a sofa that hadn't been there before with Carl piled helplessly on his back.

Vivian

Carl's wife, Vivian, was Jim's lab partner in chemistry class at Kilgore Jr. College. Carl related to me that she often told him how when they did lab work, she handled the glassware and the fire, but Jim did all the calculations in his head. She was amazed at his quickness and accuracy with math.

Lyle

Another of Jim and Carl's friends was Lyle. Lyle had cerebral palsy from a birth accident and had an extremely difficult time walking, talking, or controlling the motions of his hands and arms, yet like Jim, he refused to accept pity from anyone for his condition. His dad was a rancher, and he was a rancher. He drove a truck that was especially prepared for him. He worked cattle and attended college on his own. He even designed and had built a special box that contained his typewriter with strings attached to the keys and extending out of the front of the box where they were tied to drawer pulls. Though he lacked the dexterity to type with his fingers, he could pull the strings and manipulate the keys, allowing him to type his own papers.

They spent many days together and went places together, and I believe that Jim could see clearly the marvelously unique person inside of Lyle that refused to be dominated by the physical problems which plagued him. He had an indomitable spirit, and I believe this is what made him such a good friend to Jim.

I recently ran across Lyle and he was still driving for himself, but due to degenerating health is no longer ranching. He was still working to support himself by greeting people at the Wal-Mart in a nearby town. We reminisced about his friendship with Jim at Kilgore Jr. College and Lyle recalled how much he enjoyed listening to Jim play his guitar and sing.

FRITZ AND THE BLINK: AN OVERTURE TO LIFE

Marie

Another of Jim's friends in high school was Marie. Marie was born without thumbs on either hand, yet she never let that stop her from becoming an excellent pianist. She and Jim were the musicians for their Sunday school department and spent many hours on the phone each week planning their program and just plain shooting the bull. Because of their association with respect to church, Marie would call Jim, "St. James." Jim in turn referred to Marie as "St. Marie."

Thank You All

All of you folks and many others were special people in Jim's life. You were all special for the love you had in your hearts and the uncommon quality of knowing that pity was not allowed to be a part of your friendship. I hope that each of you will read this book and enjoy reliving the times you shared with Jim.

I have no doubt that there are more stories out there I have never been told, but I hope that those stories that remain in the minds and hearts of Jim's special friends will be retold when they can be used to inspire others to do their best for themselves.

Jim did not go out of his way searching for other handicapped persons to be his friends; he just met them as he traveled through life, the same as any of us do. The big difference with Jim was that he was not distracted by the other person's appearance or handicap as we who can see so often are; rather he had a clear, unfettered view of the heart and spirit of the person inside.

— Chapter 15 —
Don't You Laugh When the Hearse Goes By

The title of this chapter comes from the opening lines of a song Jim and I sang as kids. We were invincible; life was for living, enjoying, and savoring. As in *The Dead Poet's Society* we sucked the marrow out of the bones of life. We were taught from a very early age that death was merely a transition from living on earth to living in Heaven and was a natural part of our existence. We never gave the matter much thought when we were young. Certainly it never crossed our minds when we were attempting some new stunt we had dreamed up, like swinging on a rope over a twenty-foot deep ditch, or sliding on our shoes on a rain slicked oil road while holding on to the bumper of a car. Jim and I had a charmed childhood, neither of us ever had a broken bone or a cut requiring stitches due to any of our stunts the entire time we were growing up, though we did earn our fair share of bruises, scrapes, cuts, and sprains. It never occurred to us that anything could ever interfere with our lust for life.

This Wasn't the Way I Planned It

In late March of 1966, while Jim was a junior at Baylor University, he developed a swelling in the left side of his throat. First diagnosed and treated as mononucleosis, the swelling did not subside. Further, tests revealed that the lymph nodes in his throat were malignant with a form of cancer that was very aggressive and had already begun to spread to other lymph nodes in his body. Radiation treatments were employed, but the spread had been too rapid to confine successfully.

FRITZ AND THE BLINK: AN OVERTURE TO LIFE

As with everything else in his life, Jim took this in stride, determined to battle it with all the spirit he had, but within three months the cancer had spread wildly and begun to take its toll on Jim's health and strength. He began to lose weight and energy, but never his faith or determination. Not once did he complain about his condition as being unfair or question, as so many do, why God could allow this to happen to him. He was well aware of his situation. He knew that this type of cancer was considered terminal. He knew also that he had already lived an extraordinary life. By this time, he was engaged to a wonderful young lady and as long as he was able, though he chose not marry her under the circumstances, he was determined to enjoy the time they had left together.

Fighting Back

That summer, I made many trips to Longview to take Jim to his fiancé's house and to pick him up to bring him home later. Many nights he would leave her front door in high spirits, walk to my car and collapse in the back seat from the exhaustion of maintaining his energy and spirits in her presence. In severe pain, he would endure the half-hour ride home and collapse again in his bed, determined to rest up for the next trip.

In September, I left home to begin my college studies at Texas A&M University as a freshman. Shortly after that, Jim's health began to deteriorate very rapidly. The pain of the cancer had become so intense that he had to take pain medicine in increasing strength on a very regular basis. Dad at first was opposed to the use of morphine to relieve the pain, fearing that Jim would become addicted. Our doctor counseled him that at this point, there was no hope of improvement and that the most important thing was that Jim not be allowed to suffer the excruciating pain that the cancer was producing. Dad eventually had to administer the shots himself.

Every weekend I drove home to be with the family, and every weekend the trip became harder as Jim hurt more and more and became more dependent on drugs to ease the pain. There was nothing I could do except be with my parents and share their pain.

In late September, after Jim had been confined to the hospital, he told our folks, "If I don't get out of here in the next couple of weeks, you had better go coffin shopping." It was the only time that any member of the family ever heard him refer to his situation in less than a positive tone. Mom came home from the hospital and cried for hours that day. I suppose she was facing the reality of the situation for the first time. Dad and I had several long talks that weekend.

Sworn to Secrecy

That same day, Jim called me into his room for a private discussion. He had one item of business he needed for me to take care of. He had hidden something in the pages of his Braille Bible, which he didn't want Mom or Dad to discover later because of the embarrassment it would cause. He told me to look up John 3:16, and there I would find the item. "Get rid of it!" were his instructions. It was the last lucid conversation Jim and I would have.

I left the hospital and went immediately to his room. A full Braille Bible takes up a lot of shelf space. Three shelves, each about seven feet long were needed to hold all the volumes of print. Fortunately, the covers were indexed in print as well as Braille, so I was able to find the book of John. I had to search page by page until I found the item Jim had hidden there. I took it, carried it out of the house, got in my car and drove to a back road where I threw it out of the window, fulfilling my brotherly obligation. It was this one story that I felt I could not tell until both parents had passed away, though Dad would probably have loved to hear it. By now, I am sure Jim has told him.

Relieved of Pain

I was home that weekend in mid-October when Dad woke me up late in the night. With just two words, he let me know that our world had changed. "Jim's gone," he said calmly, choking back his emotion. I sat up quickly, and we hugged and cried. Then Mom came in and we hugged and cried. I would not cry again for nearly six months, because during that period anytime I would think of Jim, it would be to remember things we had done that had made our lives special. There was too much joy, two many good times, too many rich memories to spend any time thinking of the loss.

We Still Laughed Together

I was only eighteen and had never had to be part of the preparation of a funeral before. Jim's comment about going coffin shopping still was fresh in my mind when Mom, Dad and I went to the funeral home to take care of that item of business. I don't know if I was still in a state of denial, shock or disbelief. Maybe the memory of Jim's humor and attitude had just taken over my mind. Outside I was maintaining the necessary somber countenance required by that situation, but inside I was seeing the humor of the situation, as if Jim were by my side, cracking jokes.

We were led into a room filled with caskets and given a sales pitch, very somberly, of course, about the qualities and shortcomings of each different model. Wood caskets of pine, oak, and other more exotic woods. Each had a brochure explaining the quality and workmanship. I knew that this was not a decision I wanted be making, and in sort of a daydream, I began discussing the merits of these fine products with Jim in my mind. We were shown metal caskets, with stainless steel, copper, bronze and aluminum exteriors. *Which tin can do you prefer?* I asked Jim in my mind.

"This one has satin lining. This one has a coil spring mattress," the salesman continued. I couldn't believe what I was hearing. I knew if Jim were there, he would be laughing that deep belly laugh of his. "This model has a seal that is guaranteed not to leak for seventy-five years." Jim would have wanted to know, *"Just how they would check on that? Would they put a phone in the casket, so I could* call a repairman if it started to leak? Or perhaps they would dig it up periodically and inspect it."

"Of course, you will want to have a concrete vault to protect the casket."

"Why is that?" Jim whispered loudly in my ear. *"Didn't he just say it wouldn't leak for seventy-five years?"*

The casket Mom and Dad settled on cost just about the same as my new 1966 Mustang had cost. I remember thinking to myself that Jim would have probably liked to be buried in a Mustang, sitting behind the steering wheel, a big smile molded on his face and his arm out the window; waving goodbye as he was lowered into the hole. *"Bye, ya'll! I'll be 'seeing' you."* Years later, I heard of a Dallas millionaire who was buried in a Cadillac. It made me recall that day all over again.

One Last Scooter Ride

The funeral was enormous. Jim had many, many friends and we had a large family. One member of our family who had a little problem with mental retardation provided the comic relief; that little tension reliever that is needed at overly somber occasions. Because of his condition, Dad's cousin Leonard had never been able to get a license to drive a car, so he was obliged to drive a motor scooter to get around. Mom, Dad and I left the chapel in the family limousine at the front of the procession to the cemetery. Suddenly, Leonard passed several cars in the procession and rode right up beside the limousine. Right outside our window, he sounded his horn, grinned and waved at us before accelerating noisily past us to be the first at the gravesite. I know Jim would have appreciated that, because when we were kids Leonard would take us for rides on his scooter when he came to visit.

FRITZ AND THE BLINK: AN OVERTURE TO LIFE

Scooter Ride

JOHN R. COHAGEN

The Fat Lady Sang Before the First Act Was Over

And so, the curtain came down on Jim's opus, but not on his legacy. He left behind memories that will remain in the hearts of those who knew him until all of us have joined him. He lived a life that has been inspiration to many people and an example of getting the most out of what God gave you. He helped many people understand the meaning of perseverance, determination and faith. He taught people that it is not what happens to you, but how you react to it that counts. Most of all, I thank Jim for teaching me that it is not physical appearances or attributes than count in people, but what they are in their hearts.

A Post Script

Remember Mrs. Nixon, the Avon lady who lived across the street? After Jim's death, she saw me one day in front of the house and invited me over to her house to talk. She poured me a glass of wine. I was only eighteen, not of legal age in those days, but I sipped the wine with her and we talked about Jim. I recounted the story of how we had bombarded her from the backyard many years ago and we laughed about it. I came to understand that day that she really wasn't a pest, just a lonely widow who loved the people she knew.

— Chapter 16 —
The Other Side of the Story

While in the final stages of writing this book, I took the time to look up and visit with some of Jim's dearest friends in an effort to fill in some of the missing periods of his life. Once Jim started to college, the amount of time that we spent together decreased drastically. He had new friends, they had transportation, and I was busy with my high school activities and dating. I was sure that there had to be stories out there I had not heard yet, and I needed a few more facts and stories to complete the story I wanted to tell.

One such visit with Carl Barber, one of Jim's closest friends at Kilgore Jr. College, proved to be a gold mine of information and memories, but more significantly, it became the inspiration for this chapter. Many of the things we talked about were already included in earlier chapters and retold as a part of Jim's college years. Carl and I agreed that Jim's story needed to be told because it could serve as an inspiration to so many people who had never had the opportunity to meet Jim but who face similar trials by what life had given them. Those who had known Jim had already been touched by his courage and determination to live life to its fullest. My hope was to preserve the story of his incredible life and share it with those who might benefit from reading it.

Then Carl made a much more interesting statement, one that I had never considered as important when I began writing this book. He told me that I should also give my side of the story, the feelings and thoughts I had growing as the little brother of a very "special" person. My eyes watered and a lump formed in my throat for I had never had anyone genuinely express to me that they ever considered the role I had played in Jim's life or how our association had affected me. Carl went on to say that even as a "scatter-brained college student" he had been aware of and sensitive to how I must have felt during those years. He knew it could not have been pleasant for me always being compared to my older brother who had such a dynamic personality. Then Carl totally pierced my soul when he added that Jim had discussed this concern with him on more than one occasion.

I must admit that as I sat in Carl's office that day, tears rolled from my reddened eyes. This was the very first time in my fifty-four years that I had ever had someone actually let me know that my feelings during those years had even crossed their minds. It brought back painful memories of the feelings I had experienced with regard to my relationship with Jim, my parents and other people during that period of my life.

So, Carl, when you read this book, I want you to know how much I hate you and love you. I hate you for getting me to relive the painful memories of my life and recall them each and every time I re-read and edited this chapter. I have shed many tears over the last two years. I love you for forcing me to deal with these feelings and to finally gain closure on some feelings that I have harbored for the last thirty-six years and more. Thank you for being a true friend. Like Ebenezer Scrooge, I hope that the changes that have occurred have not come too late.

This chapter I dedicate to you in appreciation for the peace you helped me discover.

Every Life Affects Many Others

All of the preceding chapters of this book have dealt with the life of my brother and the wonderful times we had together. I still recall all the fun and adventures we had together with much joy, seasoned by the time that has since passed. Looking back at the "good old days" is easy because we tend to view the past through rose-colored glasses and highlight those times of joy and happiness we like to

FRITZ AND THE BLINK: AN OVERTURE TO LIFE

remember. However, all was not as happy as the events I recounted in the stories of our youthful lives. There was, as Carl had so aptly noted, another side of this story and after much introspection, I agree that it should be shared. So what follows is the story of the inner feelings of the little brother who grew up in the shadow of the amazing accomplishments and dynamic personality of the sibling that preceded him.

I have rewritten this chapter at least four times; each time looking deeper into myself, each time reliving pain I had forgotten, and each time gaining new insight into how subtle things had shaped me into the man I had become. I do not recount these feelings in the hope that I will receive pity, but I hope that through this effort, I will receive the peace that comes from understanding. My hope is that what I have to say about myself will be useful to the other brothers and sisters in this world who find themselves in a similar situation and help them understand the emotions they might feel when having to share their world with a "special" person. I also hope that this might help parents who find themselves in a similar situation to be able to recognize the feelings that their children might experience and search for ways handle it that are less problematic to their children than it was with me.

Jim was three years my elder, so by the time I was old enough to walk and talk, he was preparing to leave for the school in Austin. For the next eight years, we would only be "summer brothers" with a few opportunities to visit on holidays. The rest of the time, I was, for all practical purposes, an only child. Mom started her teaching career the same year I was born, and as I told you earlier in this book, our colored maid was raising me on a daily basis. Her son was my primary playmate and surrogate brother until I started kindergarten.

In the early years, I loved summers with my real brother and willingly shared *my* parents with him for the summer. We played together. We rode tricycles together on the street in front of the house. Jim taught me to read and I looked up to my big brother, as all little brothers tend to do. I was sad when summer ended and I no longer had a brother to share my bedroom with and giggle with until we fell asleep. Summers were fun because we always took a two-week vacation trip to explore the rest of the United States and experience new things, people and places.

In 1954, Jim started the fifth grade and was invited to be on the wrestling team. The following summer was somehow different. Instead of being just a little brother, I now was his wrestling "partner," or at least practice dummy. Jim loved wrestling and liked to practice with me on a quilt spread on the thick San Augustine grass in the backyard. I was much smaller and often got twisted too far by Jim in his exuberance to show me his best moves. My crying was always met with the same response by my parents, "Jim didn't *mean* to hurt you! Take it a little easier, Jimmy," but he never did because he enjoyed making me squeal. I guess it was the first resentment I had of having him around.

I never thought of my brother as handicapped, only blind. The two are not interchangeable concepts. Jim had been blind since before I was born, so I never knew he was supposed to be any other way. The word "handicap" was certainly never mentioned in any of our conversations. He could run through the house almost as fast as I could and knew every nook and cranny of our ever-growing house. We loved to play hide and seek and the many closets, pantries and storage areas offered more than ample hiding places. Jim had the advantage though because he could hear me breathing ten feet away.

About the only concession I made to his blindness was when we went walking or exploring. I was trained, not overtly, but through experience, to be a great seeing-eye brother. I was very aware of the type of things that would trip or harm Jim if he bumped into them, and we had developed silent signals to indicate to him when we were coming to steps or curbs or low clearance obstacles. I learned early that I did not hold on to him and lead, rather he would lightly touch my arm in the inside of my upper arm and would follow my movements. That way he could let go of me anytime he wished and, therefore, was not "under my control" but as independent as he wished to be. This was very important point to him and he was extremely touchy about it. Any attempt to take hold of his hand or arm was met with immediate disengagement.

I guess the real change in our loving relationship started when he decided to move back home and attend public school. I was going into the sixth grade, and he was starting high school as a freshman. My bedroom was no longer large enough for both of us, so the garage was closed in and Jim was given a room of his own. He had his own door to the outside world and a door with a privacy lock separating him from the rest of the family. My room on the other hand was next to my parents' bedroom and was a main traffic thoroughfare in our circular house. I think I was somewhat jealous of his privacy and saw it as a special treatment favoring him on the part of my parents.

Since we had always been treated so equally when we were growing up, it was hard to accept the changes that occurred that year. Jim was making new friends at school and going places that I was not allowed to go because I was still in elementary while Jim was in high school. I had always gone everywhere with Jim in the past and being excluded really hurt. I don't think that my parents were aware of my feelings, and they took for granted that I was not affected by these changes. The lack of a reasonable explanation by my parents for the changes, and my perception that they couldn't really understand my feelings about it, made it harder to accept. I began to feel in my heart that my parents loved Jimmy more than me. I know now that it was not that they loved him more, but that they understood his need to develop his independence and that necessitated their action. I wish they could have and would have taken the time to explain that better to me at the time. No youngster is willing to accept the old explanation, "your brother (sister) is older" as a rational explanation for anything. I wish my parents had been as sensitive to my needs and feelings as they were to Jim's, but I was "normal" and should have been able to understand, but I was only twelve and did not.

I'm Just Me

The next problem grew out of Jim's popularity and abilities. He had a very high IQ (somewhere over 140) and a "photographic memory." He excelled at everything he did, partly because of his intelligence but mainly due to his desire to be the best at anything he did to show he was not "handicapped." When I finally moved up to Jr. high, Jim's achievements preceded me, and if I did less than perfectly, I would be confronted with comments from my teachers like, "Jimmy did that so well, so you should be able to, also." I hated that. I was struggling desperately to develop my own personality, self-esteem and independence while being constantly compared to my older brother. It was almost more than I could take. I quickly became very bitter toward those teachers who would express that comparison and often I would quite rudely let them know that "I AM NOT JIM!" I guess that I also developed a subconscious resentment for my brother due to some teachers' lack of tact and understanding of my feelings. I developed jealousy and bitterness for being made to feel inferior. Intellectually, I knew it was not his fault, but I resented him just the same.

As a result of this constant comparison, I adopted the defensive mental attitude that I would have to accept being in second place. That attitude has haunted me for the rest of my life. It affected my drive and ambition and prevented me from doing my best in all efforts. I strove to be "the best I could be," not the best. I believed that there would always be someone better than I was at anything I might attempt; therefore, I could never be "the best."

When I was thirteen, I got a Cushman Highlander motor scooter, which gave me a great deal of mobility and independence. It also gave Jim and me the opportunity to go places together and rebuild our weakening relationship. He loved to ride and I loved to go, ANYWHERE.

The following year, I got my automobile driver's license and effectively became a chauffeur for Jim his senior year. I didn't mind this at all. Any excuse to drive the family car was good enough for fourteen-year-old boy. We both enjoyed the freedom and adventure and I felt useful once again. This continued through Jim's two years in college. He was dating a young lady from another city, and I got to take him there and pick him up after his date. For all the effort and inconvenience, I never received a single "thank you" from Jim. I guess he felt I was just doing what a little brother was supposed to do.

For my last three years of high school, Jim was in college and the comparisons to him slowly faded away. Jim had his friends and I had mine and his shadow faded from the high school campus. We had outgrown the importance of our age difference to a certain degree and became good friends once again. It was at the end of my senior year of high school that Jim was diagnosed as having cancer, but at that time, we thought it might be treatable. By summer we knew it was not to be so.

Watching Jim grow weaker and seeing his pain increase was very hard on me. I wasn't prepared to lose my brother so soon. It was a helpless feeling, knowing the outcome, but having no control of the game. I spent as much time as I could with Jim, helping him get his affairs in order, for he knew that he would not be around much longer. The fact that his type of cancer was usually terminal was not a topic we discussed, but we both knew.

By September, Jim was in great pain and taking large doses of opiates to relieve it. I think that by the end of September, he was just ready to get it over with, and those who loved him could only pray that his prayers would be answered soon. By the end of October, he was gone.

To this day, I feel that if he had lived to fulfill his dreams, he would have been successful in whatever he pursued and would have been an inspiration to all he met. The real shame is that he could have taught so many blind youngsters his secrets of his mobility, independence and successful attitude, but I don't know that he would have.

I Wish You Had Told Me

As for me, I would have given anything to have just once had Jim tell me before he died, *"Johnny, your have been a neat little brother. Thank you, for being there."* But that was not his way. And that, Carl, is why when you told me that you and Jim had discussed your shared concerns of my feelings as a younger brother, I sat in your office and cried like a baby. Until thirty-six years after his death I had never known that he ever considered my feelings or appreciated my contribution to his life.

Time supposedly heals old wounds, but the scars last a long time. As I grew up I began to understand the reasons for my feelings and learned to deal with them. I wish I could have had more help and understanding at the time to help me deal with the jealousy and pain that I sometimes felt.

So to the parents of a handicapped or "special" child and the brothers or sisters of that child, I present this chapter in hopes that it will help you be more sensitive to the feelings of those who feel they have to compete for your love and affection. Be aware that young minds can easily and innocently, but incorrectly, misinterpret your best attempts to share your love. Mom and Dad didn't love Jim more than me, but they did have to love him differently because of his condition. Be sensitive to *all* of your children's feelings, for a normal child is just that, a child, and not ready or prepared to understand his or her own emotions. Most importantly, love all of your children the same and make sure they know that you do by your words and your actions, for all children are "special" people, and they all have specific individual needs.

— Chapter 17 —
It Takes an Attitude, Not a Village

Jim was looking forward to voting in his first federal election in November of 1966. In March, when he turned twenty-one, he registered to vote so he would be ready for the November election. He had been a staunch supporter of Barry Goldwater in 1964 and didn't hesitate to make his political feelings known. He died less than three weeks from reaching that goal.

Jim was and would have continued to be a conservative. He strongly believed in state's rights, personal rights, self-determination, and bitterly opposed the interference of government in a citizen's daily life. He detested the liberal ideal of taking money from the hardworking American and giving it to those who chose to depend on the government for handouts. He believed that charity was a function of religion and he saw government give-away programs only as a means of buying votes, a means of keeping a large group of people slaves to the government and in debt to one particular political party for the "favors" they doled out. The result was the destruction of the desire of many to work for themselves and take responsibility for their own welfare and actions.

Jim had read George Orwell's book, *1984*, and was disturbed by it. He would comment on news stories of developing technologies and new government regulations and policies as they paralleled the premise of the book. I think he could see the growing involvement of government in everyday life and looked on that as a threat to his personal independence and freedom.

Individual Responsibility, Not Government Handouts, Create Success

Neither Jim nor our family ever collected any kind of disability or welfare income from the government for Jim's condition; I don't think it would ever have crossed our minds to do so. He believed that if you want to be independent, you must choose to be independent and live accordingly. Certain government programs did provide assistance in obtaining Braille books and recorded materials to assist with Jim's education, but no strings were attached to their use. With all he had going for him, I have no doubt he would have made it on his own and would have inspired others with handicaps to do the same. With his love for government, in its best form, I have no doubt that sooner or later Jim would have run for some public office and succeeded.

Jim died when Lyndon Johnson was President. He disliked the man immensely. He, with no sight, could see right through the Great Society rubbish that Johnson broadcast on this country like manure on a hay field. When you have to see everything with your mind instead of your eyes, your vision is less likely to be clouded by the smoke and mirrors so prevalent in politics then and now.

Jim was a person of strict morals, integrity, and loyalty to his friends. He had firm, well-founded beliefs based on careful study and observation of what life was all about. To him it was about freedom, independence and personal responsibility; the freedom to create your own world and the freedom to follow your dreams; the independence from unjust ideas and controls, and the independence to become what you wanted to be.

Jim also understood that all these rights and privileges came with the personal responsibility for your actions and responsibility to others with whom you had contact, and he knew you had to have respect for the freedom and independence of others to deserve the same for yourself. Jim respected the right of others to have an opinion different from his own. He often noted that everyone was entitled to an opinion, no matter how stupid it was. He certainly would have scoffed the new liberal idea that we must be tolerant and accept all other opinions as having equal value to our own. And the modern relativism would never have been accepted by Jim who understood that there is right and wrong as defined by the Creator and that we do not get to re-shape spiritual truths to fit our personal whims and opinions.

Because Jim could not see, he, on occasion, had to trust others who could. Excuse the pun, but he had to develop a "blind trust" of those people he knew well. Those people, however, had to earn his respect before he would instill that trust in them, and I cannot recall an incident where that trust was broken by him or his friends.

Jim had a great attitude about his situation and left behind a few lessons that I would like to pass on as a way to handle whatever life throws your way.

Lesson #1 — A person with a handicap is not a freak or a monster, just a person who is different. Different is neither good nor bad; it is just different. Jim remembered how in second grade, visitors who came to see the School for the Blind often visited his classroom. They were usually students from seeing schools in the area. He was really disturbed that most of the visitors would be afraid to talk to the blind students, as if they believed that they might catch something contagious. He always felt that he was being "observed" by them as if they were looking at animals at the zoo or "freaks" at the circus sideshows. It was this attitude that Jim referred to earlier when he mentioned that the hardest thing about meeting new people was for them to get used to him. In his typing class, Jim wrote a short story as an exercise showing that different was sometimes good. Fortunately, it was saved in my mother's memory box.

Irony Plays Its Hand

"Most people have heard of the monkey in the zoo who looked at the people and wondered what they were doing there. He wonders who is the funniest. During my eight

years at the Texas State School for the Blind I had a chance to see what the monkey feels like.

"It was the policy of the school to admit visitors to the school at almost any time. They were taken on guided tours of the classrooms where they were shown how things were done in the school. Many interesting things happened on these tours such as the questions that we were asked and the answers some of them got. One of the most interesting experiences I ever had with the visitors, however, was the time that Irony played its hand.

"A whole group of kids had come from one of the schools in the area to visit the school. It wasn't a very good day for doing anything; besides the cold, rain and a chilling wind made the day even more unendurable, but this didn't stop the visitors. Everything went fine for them; they were taken to several of our classrooms, shown some of the methods that are used in the school, and allowed to ask questions when we were through. At last they went down stairs to see our piano tuning department and the gym. I've never found out exactly why, but at this point their guide left them to go check on something. There they were stranded down in our basement when all of a sudden a crash of lightning struck near the building and the electricity went out all over the campus. A friend of mine and I were doing some cleaning work down in the piano tuning department and were just passing by the group with a bucket of water when one of them asked us if we could show them the way out of the building. They had to leave in about ten minutes, they explained, and their guide hadn't shown up. So my friend and I, both as blind as the proverbial bat, took the visitors out of the building and as far as I know, they got back to their school without further mishap."

FRITZ AND THE BLINK: AN OVERTURE TO LIFE

The opposite end of that spectrum for him was the person who rushed to "help" the "poor handicapped person" out of some misguided belief that it was their "duty" to help the less fortunate. Jim was neither helpless nor less fortunate. It irritated him to no end for anyone to exhibit that attitude toward him. I had one girlfriend who Jim detested because of her condescending manner toward him. She could never get use to the idea that he didn't require or want special treatment from her. When she was in the room with him, her voice and personality would change; the way some people forget how to speak adult English when they are around a baby.

Those people who helped Jim the most were those who could overlook his blindness almost entirely and be a true friend first. Only then were they able to understand when help was wanted or needed. Only then were they able to give that help out of friendship and love and not out of pity or charity. Only then was their help cheerfully accepted.

Lesson #2 — Pity is not allowed. Pity is wasted time wishing for what you can't have instead of utilizing what you do have to its maximum. For Jim, his loss of sight was less of a problem than it might be for someone who may have lost his or her sight later in life. He had no memories of ever seeing anything and, therefore, had nothing to miss. You are what you are, and you will become what you make of yourself. No one owes you a thing just because you have a problem. Jim's response to pity was ridicule, whether it was another handicapped person asking for pity or a "normal" person trying to give it.

Jim recounted in his own story that pity is the greatest handicap that a handicapped person must overcome. He cited an incident that occurred while he was in the school for the blind when a new student arrived, I think in the fifth grade. He had lost his eyes to an accident with a blasting cap. The new student felt sorry for himself for the situation he was in and bemoaned the fact he was now blind. Jim and some of his friends undertook a siege on that young man, intentionally attacking him verbally when he sought pity. Within a few weeks, pity was no longer sought and the lad was able to accept his situation and move on. Jim did not enjoy that incident, but he knew it was the first and toughest obstacle the boy had to overcome in dealing with his handicap.

Lesson #3 — A handicap is just an inconvenience and not a problem unless you choose to make it one. As his friend, "Van" told him, "To not see with your mind is far worse than to not see with your eyes." Jim's mind contained a wealth of visions. Visions of the past and visions for the future and he had an atlas of maps in his head to guide him through all the places he needed to go. Most of all, Jim had a vision of what he wanted out of life and how he was going to get there. It mattered little to him that many thought his dreams were unrealistic for a blind person. He was not going to settle for being a blind person in the traditional sense; he was going to succeed in breaking the "blink barrier."

In that regard, I believe that Jim would have viewed the Americans with Disabilities Act (ADA) and all the regulations that it has imposed on our society with much disdain. Jim's dream and goal was to be able to adapt to the world as it was and to succeed in it on his own worth. I believe that the very idea that the world had to change to meet his needs would have gone against everything he believed about himself and his ambition for success. As a "handicapped" person, Jim had a choice. He could accept the situation he was in and become a good little unfortunate "blink", or he could face every new challenge that presented itself to him with the determination to do it himself, even if it went against all conventional wisdom. He didn't want to change the world to suit him; he wanted to change himself to succeed in the world because he liked the world as it was, especially the United States of America. After all, it is known as the land of opportunity and all he wanted was the opportunity to succeed on his own merits and abilities, not through government handouts, charity or pity.

As I sit here and ponder that last statement, I believe there are many people in this country who could improve their lives and the lives of others, if they only shared that belief and pursued it with the energy that Jim did.

Lesson #4 – You never give up. Jim detested handicapped people, or anyone else, who would give up too easily when faced with a new problem. In his own words, *"Even a person who fails at a task after trying deserves more credit than one who does not try."* Sure, Jim had failures in his life, but usually it was because he set his goals higher than his current skill level would allow, but anything that he failed at became a challenge to overcome, not a reason to quit.

Lesson #5 — If you are handicapped, you must learn to be patient with the "normal" people you meet. Jim always said that the hardest part of meeting new people was their getting accustomed to him, not the other way around. Strangers did not know exactly how to talk to Jim. They were always overly cautious about what they said in fear that they might make reference to his handicap. It was generally up to him to "desensitize" the relationship by using off-handed references to his blindness to assure the new person that it was not a sensitive area, merely a fact of life that he had fully accepted and that they needed to do the same. At the same time, he did not like to talk about his blindness, or explain how it was to be blind. His blindness was simply a fact, not a topic for conversation. Even in our relationship as brothers, I can only remember maybe two occasions where we had discussions about the subject. The rest of the time we were too busy enjoying life to get into such useless discussions.

The converse of this lesson is also true. If you are not handicapped, you need to learn to be patient with and truly interested in understanding the feelings of those persons you meet who are. They didn't choose to be handicapped and appear different and would prefer that it were not so. God is not punishing them by inflicting them with this disability, nor did he make them this way so that we could have someone to feel sorry for or to make fun of. They are people with individual personalities, emotions and feelings who deserve the same respect that we might afford any other person.

Lesson #6 – When walking in a strange place, lead with your feet. Carl reminded me of this lesson. It was one that he had learned from Jim. If you have to walk in the dark in an unfamiliar place, you don't want your face to be the first thing to find a wall. Jim's normal stride, when walking in places where he was familiar with his surroundings, was much the same as yours and mine. But when Jim was walking alone on unfamiliar ground, he would hold his head back and bend his knees slightly so that his feet advanced farther forward than usual to detect obstacles before his body and head reached them. Carl told me that he had occasion to use that lesson in a pitch-black garage and found it useful.

Lesson #7 – Don't forget the little guy! This lesson was strongly implanted in my brain, not by action, but by omission. Jim was so independent and self-reliant that I think he truly hated getting help from people, though there were times that it was necessary. I was very aware of that part of his makeup and never forced my help on him. On the other hand, the person receiving help must not let his desire for independence and self-reliance overpower the need to acknowledge what people do for them, especially when those things are being done because of a true love and desire help the person succeed.

For me this was Jim's one true shortcoming. Because we were so close and grew up together, he simply took it for granted that I was supposed to do things for him. His failure to acknowledge or express gratitude for the things I did so willingly, left a scar in my soul that hurts to recall to this day.

— Epilogue —

Our memories of childhood and youth are bathed in the things we treasure in our hearts. We can look back with fondness now at even the most frightening or tragic events and glean some joy from them. The "good old days" we love to remember are gone, never to return. Maybe they never really existed at all except in our minds, but as long as they are our memories they can be relived, embellished, and enjoyed again and again.

To that end, I wrote this book. I wanted to save these memories not only for you, the reader, but also for my children and grandchildren so they might have a record of a part of their family history and the very special person with whom I shared part of my life. Before the memories died with this old body, I wanted to recall them, embellish them (maybe a little bit), and record them to share with all those who like to remember their own childhood, maybe not exactly as it was, but in the way we like to believe it was.

In the twenty-one years Jim lived, his life touched many people and inspired many more. In memory of his life, his courage, and the times and town in which we grew up, I penned this book. I hope I have done his memory justice.

About the Title of the Book

Originally the title for this book was just *Fritz and the Blink*, so named for my high school nickname and Jim's term for a totally blind person. The book was about fifty percent completed when I was able to locate Jim's high school autobiography, *An Overture to Life*. I chose at that time to incorporate the title that Jim had chosen to describe his preparation for life. After all, without his life, I would have had nothing to write about in the first place.

Conclusion

Jim's opus was cut short, like Beethoven's unfinished symphony, and like Beethoven's unfinished work, it was a masterpiece. The overture projected the anticipation for great things to come, and the first act began to set the stage that would have shown that our anticipation was justified. Unexpectedly, the fat lady sang and the curtain came down before the play could even reach scene two of the first act. Maybe this is exactly what God had in mind for Jim's life. He was not to be an example to follow for the long, successful life he might have lived, but an inspiration to those who knew him, or may come to know him through this book, for the way he faced life as it was given to him. Maybe his purpose was to be an inspiration to us, the living, for what we might believe he could have been because of his refusal to accept any limitations imposed by his handicap. Had he lived and failed to meet our expectations, he would have lost his importance as an inspiration. Maybe that helps explain why I was compelled to write this book to preserve and extend the memory of his inspiring life.

This is my gift to you, Jim, the memory of your life that will be extended until I get to meet you again in a place that will be so much better. When we meet, I will no longer be old and fat and you will not be blind. We will enjoy the perfection of God's love and have eternity to look back on the wonderful times we shared for eighteen years on earth. I'm sure that those around us will laugh, too, as we recall the details that I have already forgotten. Of course, in Heaven, we cannot lie about what we did, but maybe we can still stretch the truth just a little.

FRITZ AND THE BLINK: AN OVERTURE TO LIFE

I am reminded of a song that Jim sang in his youth about being in heaven. All the words I cannot recall, but the ending went something like this:

I saw Peter, Paul and Moses
Playing ring around the roses,
And I'll whip the man that says it isn't so.

That always conjured up such an image in my mind of the joy of Heaven, a place where we will enjoy eternity with the same innocence and joy of children as they play together.

The Curtain Falls

So there you have it. While writing this book, I stirred up emotions and memories both happy and sad from my own life. Many tears have run down my cheeks during the writing and editing. If I have stirred your memories or your emotions, then I have accomplished my purpose and goal. Every time you recall one of these stories, you will help perpetuate the life of a very special brother and friend, for as Mom always taught us,
"As long as you live in the memory of another, you never die."

So for now we must visit here
until we meet again.

Printed in the United States
26006LVS00001B/235-282